WOMAN SPELLED TROUBLE—THREE WAYS

Ella had known every kind of man and knew just how to please in every kind of way—at a price Cimarron discovered too late to say no.

Lila was a farm girl who learned everything about the birds and the bees and nothing about men—until Cimarron yanked the rifle from her hands and gave them something better to do.

For Belle, a man was something to be used for whatever she happened to want—and she used every inch of everything Cimarron had, from his manhood to his gun.

Cimarron was riding on the other side of the law—through a trackless territory where no man could be trusted and the female of the species was even deadlier than the male. . . .

CIMARRON
RIDES THE OUTLAW TRAIL

SIGNET Westerns You'll Enjoy

2. CIMARRON
RIDES THE OUTLAW TRAIL

by
LEO P. KELLEY

A SIGNET BOOK
NEW AMERICAN LIBRARY
TIMES MIRROR

PUBLISHER'S NOTE

This novel is a work of fiction. Names, characters, places, and incidents either are the product of the author's imagination or are used fictitiously, and any resemblance to actual events or persons, living or dead, is entirely coincidental.

NAL BOOKS ARE AVAILABLE AT QUANTITY DISCOUNTS WHEN USED TO PROMOTE PRODUCTS OR SERVICES. FOR INFORMATION PLEASE WRITE TO PREMIUM MARKETING DIVISION, THE NEW AMERICAN LIBRARY, INC., 1633 BROADWAY, NEW YORK, NEW YORK 10019.

The first chapter of this book appeared in CIMARRON AND THE HANGING JUDGE, the first volume in this series.

SIGNET TRADEMARK REG. U.S. PAT. OFF. AND FOREIGN COUNTRIES REGISTERED TRADEMARK—MARCA REGISTRADA HECHO EN CHICAGO, U.S.A.

SIGNET, SIGNET CLASSICS, MENTOR, PLUME, MERIDIAN AND NAL BOOKS are published by The New American Library, 1633 Broadway, New York, New York 10019

First Printing, February, 1983

1 2 3 4 5 6 7 8 9

PRINTED IN THE UNITED STATES OF AMERICA

CIMARRON . . .

. . . he was a man with a past he wanted to forget, and a future uncertain at best and dangerous at worst. Men feared and secretly admired him. Women desired him. He roamed the Indian Territory with a Winchester .73 in his saddle scabbard, an Army Colt in his hip holster, and a bronc he had broken beneath him. He packed his guns loose, rode his horse hard, and no one dared throw gravel at his boots. Once he had an ordinary name like other men. But a tragic killing forced him to abandon it, and he became known only as Cimarron. *Cimarron,* in Spanish, meant wild and unruly. It suited him. *Cimarron.*

Cimarron dragged the pine saplings he had felled out of the grove of trees. He began to haul them toward the southern edge of the encampment of United States deputy marshals that was sprawled on the western bank of the Arkansas River.

As he passed canvas army tents and crude lean-tos, he was only half-conscious of the sounds that the other deputies in the camp were making because he was thinking about Sarah Lassiter.

The clang of a horseshoe as it hit the iron spike that had been driven into the ground rang in the early June morning's still and humid air. A man shouted. Another swore. Another clang sounded and it was quickly followed by a loud argument between two men who were bending over the spot near the spike where the thrown horseshoe had landed.

She's gone, Cimarron thought, as he slapped at a mosquito that had landed on his neck. He used three of the saplings to form a wide-based tripod after lashing them together at one end with rawhide. He wondered if he'd ever see Sarah Lassiter again. He hoped he would. And he might. She lived just northwest of Tahlequah, the capital of Cherokee Nation, and Tahlequah, he knew, wasn't a very long ride from Fort Smith, the frontier town that squatted on the other side of the Arkansas.

A man shouted—a name. There was an answering shout. Then booming laughter from several throats.

They had spent three days together, Cimarron and Sarah, in the small and none-too-clean hotel in Fort

Smith. Yesterday she had returned to the female seminary she had been attending just northwest of Tahlequah.

But to Cimarron it seemed like it had been weeks since he had seen—had gently touched and eagerly held—her. Thinking of those arousing nights—and days—that they had spent so happily together in the big brass hotel bed brought a smile to his face.

Someone in the camp behind him snickered as he leaned more poles against the top of the tripod and then began covering them with a tarpaulin.

He used wooden pegs he had whittled to fasten the tarpaulin to the ground and then he ducked down and went inside the tepee he had built and gripped the length of rawhide that dangled from the top of the tripod and lay in a coil on the grassy ground.

He pounded another wooden peg into the ground directly beneath the apex of the tripod with one booted foot and then tied the rawhide tightly to the peg to keep the tepee stable in even the strongest wind.

"Ain't a tent good enough for you?" someone asked, and Cimarron glanced over his shoulder to find Deputy Marshal Pete Smithers peering into the dim interior of the shelter.

"Don't happen to have a tent, Smithers," Cimarron replied amiably. "Nor do I have the wherewithal to buy myself one."

He left the tepee, shouldering Smithers out of his way as he did so, and proceeded to insert the ends of two saplings in the small pockets he had made in the top of the tarpaulin in order to control the makeshift smoke flaps he had fashioned there.

Smithers, a wooden toothpick between his lips, said, "You wouldn't happen to be part Injun, now would you be, Cimarron?"

"Might be. My pa, he was a wandering man. There's just no telling what he might have gotten himself into in his traveling down in Texas." Cimarron gave Smithers a smile, unbothered by the lie he had just told—more of a joke on himself than a genuine lie—and then tested the two poles, opening and closing the smoke flaps.

"You mean *who* he might have gotten himself into, don't you?" Smithers asked with a sly grin.

Cimarron anchored the smoke-flap poles in place and then turned around. He studied Smithers for a moment—the man's mirthless grin, his feral eyes, his smooth, faintly pink complexion.

Smithers said, "That there thing you just put up, it looks a whole lot like an Injun house to me. That's why I asked if you were part Injun." He paused, his eyes on Cimarron, before adding, "That and the fact that I heard you were living over in the hotel in town with a Cherokee squaw."

"What people hear," Cimarron said, "is more often than not best left unrepeated."

"You hold anything against your own kind?" Smithers asked. "I mean against white women?"

"Smithers, don't you have enough business of your own to mind without mixing yourself up in mine?"

"How was she, Cimarron? I hear some of those squaws are awful eager to snuggle up tight against big and brawny white bucks like you. Was she good?"

Cimarron sighed. "Miss Lassiter is no concern of yours, Smithers. Nor am I."

Smithers slapped his thigh and hooted. "You hear him, fellas?" he called out to the other deputies in the camp. "Touchy sort, now ain't he just?"

"I'm going to ask you real polite, Smithers," Cimarron said in a low tone as several idly curious deputies wandered over to join the pair. "I'm asking you to let it lie, Smithers."

"You fellas heard about this here squaw man?" Smithers asked the deputies, and without waiting for a reply, continued, "This old Cimarron just barely manages to slip his neck out of Maledon's noose last month and before you can say 'God made little green apples' he slipped his—"

Cimarron's right hand shot out and seized Smithers by the throat, cutting off the man's words. With his left hand he unbuckled Smithers' gun belt and tossed it to the ground some distance away. Only then did he release Smithers and proceed to unbuckle his own gun belt from which hung the holster that housed his single-action Frontier Colt .45 from which he had cut away the trigger guard. He tossed it to the ground.

3

"Now what exactly might you have in mind?" Smithers asked him as he rubbed his throat.

"Murder for one thing," Cimarron answered. "Only I'm not a murdering man as a rule, though gents like you do sorely try the patience of a peaceful man like I usually am."

Smithers' eyes widened in mock surprise. "You want to murder me?"

Cimarron sighed again. "I'll ask you just one more time, Smithers. Let it lie."

"And if I don't?"

"You'll wish to hell and back that you had."

"You think you can take me?"

"I plan on trying my best to."

"Oh, you do, do you?" Smithers growled, discarding his hat and gnawed toothpick. "Don't see what you're all fired up about. A Cherokee squaw ain't much better than a nigger gal, you come right on down to it."

Cimarron swung. His right uppercut caught Smithers on the jaw and sent him staggering backward.

Almost immediately, Smithers regained his balance. His fists clenched. He said, "I got twenty, maybe twenty-five pounds on you, Cimarron. I'm going to pound you so far into the ground it'll take a crew with shovels to find you."

"Time for talking's past. Let's have at it."

Smithers launged, his right fist drawn back. Although Cimarron was much lighter than his opponent, he made up for his lack of bulk with a litheness that was more characteristic of a cougar than of most men. He leaned to the right and Smithers' blow glanced off his left shoulder.

He turned and brought the heel of his right fist down hard on the side of Smithers' head. Then, as the man turned toward him, Cimarron followed up with a fast left jab, sending his fist into Smithers' fleshy gut.

Smithers doubled over, gasping for air, and then, both of his fists flying wildly, he hurled himself at Cimarron.

Cimarron took a right and a left to the ribs, losing his hat in the process. He reached out and grabbed Smithers' shoulders with both of his hands. He pulled the man toward him, turned him, thrust his right leg behind Smithers' knees, and threw him to the ground.

Smithers, propping himself up on both elbows, blinked

4

up at Cimarron. Then, struggling to his feet as Cimarron stepped warily backward, he aimed a vicious kick at Cimarron's shin.

Cimarron had seen the kick coming and he shunted Smithers' booted foot aside with his own right foot.

When Smithers tried a second time to kick him in the shin, Cimarron grabbed the man's raised ankle, twisted it hard, and again Smithers hit the ground. This time, when he came up, he began to circle Cimarron, his fists raised, his eyes fiery.

Cimarron, also circling, suddenly moved in and landed a savage succession of blows to Smithers' head and body.

"Don't dance, Smithers!" one of the deputies yelled. "*Fight* the man!"

As if the words had been a sharp goad, Smithers moved in and Cimarron failed to step aside quickly enough. Smithers' fist smashed into his jaw and his head snapped backward. Recovering, he swiftly raised his left arm to ward off the next blow Smithers was throwing at him, and his knees slightly bent in order to maintain his center of gravity, he jabbed hard, avoiding Smithers' ribs and going again for the man's gut, where he knew he could do more damage.

His blow connected and the winded Smithers sagged but did not fall.

Then he lunged at Cimarron again.

Cimarron sidestepped, and as Smithers went past him, he turned, grabbed the man from behind by the shoulders. At the same time he slammed his right leg against the back of Smithers' knees and Smithers' body bent backward. Cimarron jerked hard on Smithers' shoulder; Smithers, thrown off balance, fell on his back.

Cimarron waited, sweating beneath the hot sun, his face slick.

Smithers slowly rose, his hands swinging at his sides, his chest heaving. And then he made a grab for Cimarron.

Cimarron's left fist shot out. But Smithers slapped it aside and locked both hands behind Cimarron's neck. He brought his right knee up as he bent Cimarron's head down toward the ground. It smashed into Cimarron's nose, from which blood immediately began to flood.

5

Cimarron butted Smithers with his head, sending him hopping backward and breaking the grip on his neck.

He moved in fast then, and opening his fist, his fingers outstretched and held tightly together, he gave Smithers a chopping blow to the Adam's apple.

Smithers gagged and clutched his throat.

His nose still bleeding badly, Cimarron seized Smithers, spun him around, and shot two fast fists into the small of the man's back. Before Smithers could recover from the blows, which had been meant to hurt both his lower spine and kidneys, Cimarron spun him around and threw another punch, which hammered against Smithers' chin.

Smithers retaliated with two swiftly thrown punches, and for more than a minute, they slugged it out toe to toe.

Cimarron came in under Smithers' swing and his fists began to savage Smithers' face. They opened the flesh of his left cheek and badly bruised his right eye.

Smithers staggered backward. His knees buckled under him. But he stood his ground, swaying, blinking, blood from the cut on his cheek reddening his face.

Then he lunged again, clumsily, and Cimarron gave him two short but sharp punches—a ripping right that got Smithers just below the ribs, and a stunning left uppercut that crashed against his lower jaw.

Smithers fell.

"He's about finished," one of the deputies remarked, pointing to the downed Smithers and sounding disappointed.

Smithers managed to get to his knees. He swayed drunkenly for a moment and then pitched backward into a sitting position.

Cimarron shook his head to clear it of the grogginess he was experiencing. With the back of his right hand, he wiped the blood from his upper lip. Then he untied the bandanna from around his neck and blew his nose in it, soaking it with blood in the process. His eyes still on Smithers, he gingerly felt his nose and winced in pain as he did so.

"Broken?" someone asked him.

Cimarron turned to find a deputy he didn't know standing beside him. "Don't think so," he answered. "Hope not."

"You're some fistfighter," the deputy commented, his eyes appraising Cimarron. "One of the best I've seen."

"My brother and me, when we were but knee-high to a small horse, used to go at it from time to time, more for fun than much of anything else. We each of us picked up a trick or two."

Two deputies were helping Smithers to his feet. As they led him away, the deputy beside Cimarron asked, "What started it all?"

"Deputy Smithers said some unkind words about a lady who happens to be a friend of mine."

"That'll do it every time," the deputy commented laconically. "By the way, my name's Cass Renquist."

"Cimarron."

"I know," Renquist said. "You're well-known over in Fort Smith. People talk about you. Point you out to each other."

Cimarron glared at him.

Catching the glint in Cimarron's eyes, Renquist held up his hands, palms toward Cimarron and took a step backward. "Hold on now. I'm not aiming to take you on. I figure you could do for me, even the way you're bruised and beat up some right now."

Cimarron went over to where he had dropped his gun belt. He picked it up and strapped it on, adjusting it until it hung low and easy on his hips. Then he retrieved his hat, clapped it on his head, and strode down to the river, where he knelt and rinsed the blood from his bandanna. As he stood up, Renquist joined him.

"Cimarron, Jim Fagan sent me out to look for you."

"That a fact?"

"Jim wants to see you. He's got a case he wants to send you out on."

Cimarron nodded. "It'll be my first since I was sworn in as a deputy marshal. He tell you what kind of case it is?"

"Jim said something about a witness he wants brought into town. But I'd better let him spell it out for you himself. I might get it all garbled up."

Cimarron wrung the water out of his bandanna, and as he started toward his tepee, Renquist called out to him, "Jim wants to see you as soon as possible."

Cimarron waved a hand and ducked into his tepee. He spread his bandanna out on the grass inside it and then went and got his saddle, rifle, and other gear and placed them inside the tepee.

On his way to the ferry slips, he passed Smithers, who was sitting disconsolately and alone beside his brush-covered lean-to. Neither man spoke.

Cimarron walked on, and after boarding the ferry, he stood alone on its deck, his back braced against its railing.

Cimarron was a tall man. His body was lean but solid, with broad shoulders and almost nonexistent hips. His chest was thick and his arms were strongly muscled. Now, his body bruised and aching, he stood stiffly on the deck of the ferry as the stern lines were freed by deckhands and the boat began to move out into the river, but usually he assumed an easy, almost loose stance that nevertheless gave him an air of wariness, as if he were making himself ready for anything the unpredictable world around him might have to offer.

The skin of his face had been bronzed by the sun and there were wrinkles at the corners of his eyes, the result of his having squinted long and often as he walked or rode beneath that sun. His features were strong and distinct. A square jaw. Thin lips beneath a wide-nostriled nose. Slightly sunken cheeks beneath prominent cheekbones. A broad forehead that was deeply creased.

His face was a face that showed clear signs of weathering and one that hinted of pain that had been endured because it could not be escaped.

His eyes were the color of emeralds and they were deeply set, alert; some men had, at times, found them uncomfortably keen.

A livid scar on the left side of his face began just below his eye and curved down along his cheek to end just above the corner of his mouth.

His straight black hair buried both his ears and the nape of his neck.

He had never been able to bring himself to believe that he was handsome, although there had been women in his life who had claimed he was. Just as there had been men he had known who had insisted that he looked like a man only recently escaped from hell.

8

He wore a gray flannel shirt above his jeans, which were tucked into dusty black boots that reached almost to his knees. Their toes were scuffed and their underslung heels were worn down on their outer edges. On his head he wore a battered and sweat-stained black slouch hat. His gun belt was made of untooled leather as was the holster containing his .45.

Cimarron was the first passenger off the ferry when it docked in its slip on the eastern bank of the Arkansas. He hurried past the railyards, excitement surging within him as he thought about the case Fagan was about to assign to him. What was it that Renquist had said? Something about a witness who had to be brought in to testify at a trial in Judge Parker's court. His excitement began to wane as he passed the waterfront saloons and turned left on Rogers Avenue. It didn't seem to him that bringing in a witness was much of a job for a federal lawman.

As he passed through the gate and entered the stone-walled compound of the old fort, he headed for the federal courthouse.

He took the steps leading up to it two at a time, as if he were trying to escape from the gallows that loomed so threateningly in the otherwise empty compound.

Later, as he knocked on the door of Marshal James Fagan's office, Cimarron felt his earlier excitement returning. Maybe the case would involve more than merely serving a summons on a witness. Maybe Marshal Fagan hadn't told Renquist everything about it.

"Come in!"

Cimarron opened the door of the office and stepped inside. Fagan was seated behind his desk in a big brown leather chair, and he looked up as Cimarron closed the door behind him.

"So Renquist found you," he said abruptly. "Well, don't just stand there, Cimarron. Come over here and sit down. I'll be with you in just a minute."

Cimarron crossed the room and sat down; Fagan leafed through some papers that were littering his desk and then threw them aside in evident disgust and said, "Bill Clayton has fallen into the nasty habit of giving me more work to do than ten men might be able to handle in half a lifetime."

9

"I guess the prosecutor himself's kept pretty busy," Cimarron observed, referring to Clayton.

Fagan leaned back in his chair and closed his eyes. "Seventy thousand square miles in the Indian Territory," he said softly. "And every inch of it's infested with thieves, murderers, rapists, and every other base form of humanity that crawls across the face of this sad earth of ours. No wonder this court's always so busy. No wonder Judge Parker has to hold night as well as day sessions. No wonder I sometimes feel so tired that I could drop in my tracks and let myself be trampled to death by defense lawyers without so much as whimpering."

"Renquist told me you had a case you were going to send me out on."

Fagan opened his eyes and stared dreamily at Cimarron. "What's that you said? A case?"

"Renquist said—"

"Oh, yes." Fagan shuffled among his papers, pushed them aside, pulled open a drawer of his desk, rummaged about in it for a moment, and then triumphantly sat up straight in his chair and waved a paper at Cimarron. "Here it is."

Cimarron waited, his eyes on the paper in Fagan's hand.

"You're to take this summons and ride out of here, Cimarron. Somewhere out there in the Nations is a man named"—Fagan peered at the paper in his hand—"a man named Archie Kane. You're to find him and bring him back here. Kane was an eyewitness to a horse theft. We've got the thief—his name's Dade Munrow—locked up in the jail down in the basement. But without Kane's testimony against him, Bill Clayton is convinced he'll never get a conviction."

"This Archie Kane—he's not wanted for any crime?"

Fagan shook his head. "We desperately need him as a witness for the prosecution in the case against Munrow."

"Seems to me you could send the court bailiff out on an errand like that," Cimarron said, frowning. "Maybe even the court clerk or reporter."

"See here, Cimarron," Fagan said, leaning over his desk and brandishing the summons. "You decided you wanted to be a deputy marshal for the United States Court for the Western District of Arkansas, did you not?"

"You swore me in yourself, Marshal."

"Then you must have realized by now that you take your orders from me. And the order I'm giving you right now is quite simple and straightforward. Find Archie Kane and bring him into Fort Smith." Fagan peered through narrowed eyes at Cimarron. "What the hell happened to your face?"

"Got in a fight."

"With whom?"

"Deputy Pete Smithers."

"You deputies are supposed to work together—to cooperate with each other. You're not supposed to try to kill or maim one another. Deputies are hard to find. At least, good ones are."

Cimarron said nothing.

"Bully boys!" Fagan snapped angrily. "Brawlers, every one of you! If the outlaws I send my deputies out after don't kill them, they'll probably do each other in themselves."

"Maybe you could send somebody else out after Kane," Cimarron suggested hopefully. "I wouldn't mind one bit going out after a killer. Or even a thief. But a witness? Now, that strikes me as too tame by far. I'd been hoping to find a little excitement in my new line of work."

Fagan groaned. "You'll find all the excitement you can—or maybe can't—handle out there in the territory. It'll pop up from behind every boulder and come roaring out at you from every deep draw. Believe me, I know what I'm talking about.

"I was once a deputy of this court myself and just as green as you are right now. I rode day after day and year after year through those hills and the long grass. I passed more lonely cabins and ranches than I can count. I've been in more frontier towns than I care to recollect.

"And I've been shot at. Hit a time or two. Men have come at me with knives. Women have come at me with— Never mind. I've buried friends out there. I've still got enemies out there.

"Oh, you'll find excitement in the territory all right. But until you've learned how to handle yourself in this

11

job, you'll take the easy assigments for a while. Although, I hasten to add, no assignment in the Nations can truly be called an easy assignment. The territory is a first cousin to hell."

"I was out there in the Nations," Cimarron said, wondering if Fagan might have forgotten that fact. "So I guess you're right."

"You're damned right I'm right!" Fagan exclaimed. "You ran into that jasper who was running rifles to the Kiowas—what was his name?"

"Philip Griffin."

"And his woman—that Dorset woman."

"Emma Dorset." Cimarron recalled the night he had shared a campsite with Emma and she had come to him in the middle of the night and they had . . .

"So you know what can happen to a man—lawman or not—out there or at least you ought to know by now," Fagan said, and Cimarron's thoughts of Emma Dorset fled. "Hell, you were almost hanged because of what happened to you out in the Nations last month."

Cimarron's hand went to his throat and rested there as an image of the man they called the Prince of Hangmen—of the gaunt and stony-eyed George Maledon—crossed his mind.

"Maybe you don't really want to be a deputy marshal," Fagan prodded.

"Where can I find Archie Kane?"

Fagan leaned back in his chair again. "I can't tell you where to find him."

"Then I'm supposed to fiddle-foot my way around seventy thousand square miles of country looking for a man who might be anywhere, that it?"

With his eyes still closed, Fagan said, "Two weeks ago another of my deputies served Kane with a summons to appear here in court. Kane never came in and Judge Parker was forced to postpone Dade Munrow's trial. My deputy caught up with Kane that time in Catoosa. You know where that is?"

"It's northeast of Tulsey Town, isn't it?"

"You've got it," Fagan said, opening his eyes and beaming at Cimarron. "If I were you, I'd start hunting Kane in Catoosa. Ask around about him. You might stumble on him there or on somebody who can point out his trail to you."

"If I don't run Kane to ground—if I have to come back empty-handed . . ."

"*Don't!*" Fagan said sternly, and his eyes glittered.

Cimarron nodded thoughtfully. "I'll find Kane. Bring him back."

"That's the spirit!" Fagan declared enthusiastically, beaming at Cimarron again.

Cimarron got up and started for the door.

"*Dammit,* Cimarron!"

Cimarron turned around to face Fagan. "Marshal?"

Fagan held up his hand, which still clutched the paper he had taken from his desk drawer. "The summons, Deputy. You *will* be needing it."

Sheepishly Cimarron recrossed the room and took the paper from Fagan's hand. Thrusting it into the pocket of his jeans, he made for the door and went through it.

As he left the courthouse, he avoided looking at the gallows, and once out in the town, he walked briskly through it, conscious of the stares that were being sent his way by both women and men. Passing the hotel, he found himself once again musing on the time he had spent in it with Sarah Lassiter. He supposed that the people staring surreptitiously at him all knew about that rendezvous as well as the fact that he had been convicted by a jury in Judge Parker's court and sentenced by the judge to hang. He wondered idly which event—his conviction or his having briefly shared Sarah Lassiter's bed—was considered to be the more heinous crime by the law-abiding citizens of Fort Smith.

Once back on the western bank of the Arkansas, he made his way to the deputies' encampment and his tepee.

He picked up his Winchester '73 repeater, slung his saddle over his shoulder, and carrying the rest of his gear, made his way to the western flank of the encampment, where a picket rope had been set up.

He went to his dun and proceeded to saddle and bridle the animal. He examined each one of its shoes, and satisfied that they were in good condition, he freed the animal and swung into the saddle.

Turning the horse, he rode northwest, the Arkansas on

13

his right, the lightly forested plain of the river affording him some relief from the blasting heat of the sun high in the sky above him.

As he rode, the creaking of his saddle leather beneath him was the only sound in the stillness that lay like a pall on the flood plain.

It was midafternoon when he spotted the small flock of grouse ahead of him. He reined in his dun and pulled his rifle from its saddle scabbard. He brought the rifle up and, a moment later, fired.

The grouse went winging away—all but one, which lay dead on the ground.

Cimarron cantered up to it and dismounted. Pulling his bowie knife from his right boot, he lopped off the bird's head and legs and then gutted it, after which he proceeded to remove its feathers.

He built a small fire in a circle of stones and then spitted the bird, using a branch he had broken from a willow. He sat cross-legged on the ground as he held the bird over the flames, turning it slowly. When it was evenly browned, he began to devour it, holding the spit in both hands.

When nothing of the grouse remained but a white litter of bones that lay between him and the fire, he opened his canteen and took a long drink of water. Then, after kicking out the fire, he got back in the saddle and continued his journey.

Less than an hour later, as he was approaching the foothills of the Boston Mountains, he suddenly turned his horse and galloped toward a stand of nearby aspens.

He heard the rifle shot. The bullet passed harmlessly behind him.

The rifleman, he thought as he rode in among the aspens, was a fool. Whoever it was who had shot at him from the mountains had made the mistake of skylining himself. A moment after Cimarron had spotted his unknown assailant, he had seen the glint of sunlight on the man's rifle barrel and he had wasted no time, asked himself no questions. He had merely moved and moved fast. As a direct result, he was still alive.

He slid out of the saddle and positioned himself behind

14

an aspen from which point he scanned the mountains looming in the distance. He saw no one.

Fagan, he thought grimly, had been right. Indian Territory was not a safe place to be. He knew that every outlaw west of the Mississippi had taken refuge in the territory at one time or another.

Who, he wondered, was the man who had just fired at him.

And then he asked himself an even more important question: *why* had the man fired at him?

2

Maybe he wants my horse, Cimarron thought. Or maybe my guns. Any money I might have.

He won't get whatever it is he wants, though, he vowed. He won't get me. Not if I can help it. He kept his eyes on the rolling terrain of the foothills that in places softly serrated the sky behind them. No sign of the gunman.

Gone?

There was a way to find out. Step out from behind the tree.

And take a bullet in the belly?

He took a step backward, moving away from the aspen in front of him. And then another cautious step. A third. He reached out and gripped the dun's bridle, turning the horse toward him as he continued to move deeper into the grove. Then he cut to his right, leading the dun through the trees. He began to run. When he reached the southern fringe of the grove of trees, he leaped into the saddle, crooked his left arm around his horse's neck, and slid down along the right side of the horse.

As the dun galloped south, he kept the body of the animal between him and the foothills, hoping he was out of range of the rifleman, hoping too that the man hadn't shifted south as he was doing, wondering if the man would be able to down his horse. If that happened . . .

Well, it hadn't happened. Not yet, it hadn't. No use fretting unless it did.

He reached for the bridle and turned the horse east toward the southern flank of the foothills. When he reached them, he pulled himself up in the saddle, and bending low over his horse's neck and blinking as the animal's mane blew into his eyes, he rode up the sloping ground and into the hills. When he judged that he had gone far enough, he turned north to circle around and come in behind his attacker.

When he was still some distance from the position that had been occupied by the would-be bushwhacker, he slid out of the saddle, unholstered his Colt, and left the horse, its reins trailing, behind him. Crouching, he moved west.

Several minutes later, hunkered down behind a rocky outcropping, he surveyed the land in front of him.

Empty.

Maybe.

He cocked his Colt and pulled its trigger.

There was no return fire.

Nevertheless, he waited, letting minutes pass uncounted. He watched the shadows of the clouds drift along the ground in front of him. He felt the breeze pass by him on its way to no place in particular. He listened to the world around him. Silence. Except for the faint whirring of a grasshopper on its short and seemingly erratic flights from place to place in the thick grass. No sound of bird or beast. Obviously his shot had silenced the birds and made any animal that might be nearby wary. His eyes spotted a squirrel crouched, as motionless as he himself was, on the branch of a tree where it was half-hidden by glossy green leaves.

He moved forward, still crouching, ready to hit the ground at the slightest suggestion of danger, his eyes and ears alert.

As he passed below the branch on which the squirrel perched, it didn't move. But then, as he moved on, he heard it scamper along the branch—and then silence again.

He found sign a few moments later. Flattened grass where a horse had stood and circled. Uneven stalks of grazed grass. Hoofprints of a shod horse. So his attacker probably had not been an Indian. He found the gunman's spent rifle shell.

He straightened up and looked down at the grove of aspens into which he had ridden when he had caught the glint of sunlight on the long rifle barrel. Then he slowly turned in a full circle, his eyes steady, taking in the hills and the few trees, the empty land. He identified the dips in the terrain where a man might hide. He stood rigidly, waiting again, the hammer of the Colt in his hand at full cock.

Several minutes later, he relaxed and walked slowly back to where he had left his horse, ready at the slightest sound to spin around, to fire, to kill whoever it was who had tried to kill him.

His horse tossed his head when he came into sight. It drew back its lips to reveal its bit and strings of saliva dripped from its mouth.

He picked up the reins and stepped into the saddle. He holstered his Colt and rode back the way he had just come and then down out of the hills and onto the level ground in front of them.

He rode out in the open of necessity, not worried about the fact that he presented an easy target because there was no shelter nearby from which a gunman could try to take him without being seen. The grass was short and he kept scanning it in every direction in case the mysterious gunman had managed to flatten himself upon it while he had been coming up from behind the man's former position in the foothills.

He slowed his horse when he caught sight of a dull brown patch on the ground ahead of him. But as he squinted into the sunlight, he saw that the brownness was nothing more than an expanse of grassless ground.

The cumulus clouds in the sky above him gradually dissolved as he rode on, to be replaced by the thin white streaks of cirrus clouds, which gradually thickened. Eyeing them, he knew that rain would fall sometime within the next twenty-four hours or so. He hoped he would be in Catoosa by then. Inside somewhere. He wondered if Catoosa had its share of cribs. Likely, he thought, The town had a hell-bent reputation as a watering hole for drifters, rustlers, bootleggers, highwaymen, and other assorted ruffians.

I ought to feel right at home there, he thought wryly, especially if there's women present, be they pretty or plain.

He felt a growing tautness in his groin, a faint tingling

18

sensation, as he rode on and the descending sun gilded the undersides of the wispy clouds, turning them a bright bronze.

Hunger rumbled within him, and as he remembered the grouse he had eaten earlier, he salivated. He scanned the land. No sign of animal or bird. The sun was reaching for the horizon. Was he then to go supperless? He rode on, and when he caught sight of the Illinois River up ahead of him, which was glowing golden in the dying light of the day's departing sun, he rode toward it, an idea forming in his mind.

But before he reached the river, he halted his horse and got out of the saddle. He walked toward the river leading the dun, his eyes on the ground before him. It didn't take him long to locate what he had been looking for. As his boots moved through the grass, they disturbed a grasshopper.

It flew up and away.

He saw where it had landed and he reached down and scooped up the insect. After crushing the life from it, he pocketed it, wiping on his jeans the brown juice it had spat on his hand before it died. He continued walking toward the river, his eyes still searching.

But he found no wild grapevines growing in his path that he could use to form a fishing line. He did find a stunted wild rose bush in lush June bloom, from which he broke a long thorn which he pocketed.

When he reached the riverbank, he pulled his bowie knife from his right boot and his shirttail from his jeans. Then he hunkered down and made a long cut in his shirttail. He unraveled the threads of his sliced shirttail and began to weave them together. When he had made himself a line, one he had tightly braided to give it strength, he took the dead grasshopper from his pocket along with the rose thorn. He impaled the grasshopper on the thorn, leaving the thorn's point protruding slightly from the insect's body.

Then he cut a small strip of cloth from his shirttail and some hairs from his chest. He bound the wiry black hairs to the grasshopper with the strip of blue cloth and then tied the end of his makeshift line to the equally makeshift fly he had made.

19

He tossed the line out over the water and watched it drop. He jerked it and sent the fly swirling through the water. Still hunkered down, he kept his eyes on the fly, which was dipping and darting beneath the surface of the water.

Five minutes later, he spotted a dark shadow just below the surface of the river. He pulled on his line. The fish, in pursuit of the fly, broke the surface, and he let the line lie still in the water for a moment before giving it a jerk. When it suddenly grew taut, he jerked it again, snagging the fish. He pulled hard on the line, and as he did so, the fish again broke the surface of the water, turning and twisting.

He quickly drew the fish through the water toward him and then, when it was close enough, seized it with both hands. He turned and threw it far up on the bank, the fly still in its mouth, the line trailing from it.

He climbed up on the bank and stood looking down at the grayling he had caught as it began to flop its life away in the deadly open air.

He didn't wait for it to die before slicing open the abdominal wall from anal vent to the cartilage beneath the gills. He cut off the pectoral and large dorsal fins. Then he gutted the fish, spilling its internal organs on the ground. He deftly cut out the anus, scaled the fish by scraping it from tail to head with his knife, and then sliced off both head and tail before carrying the bloody carcass to the bank, where he washed it in the river's cool water.

After building a small fire, he placed the grayling on a flat slab of rock he had found; he set it at a low angle over the flames. When the fish was baked, he stamped out the fire and let it cool slightly. Then he picked it up in both hands and began to eat it, spitting out bones and licking his lips as he did so, pleased with his supper's slightly smoky flavor.

As the sun went down, rain began to fall.

He removed his slicker from his bedroll, put it on, and resumed his journey. He found a place to ford the Illinois and then rode on, rain pouring from his hat's brim. An hour passed before the rain slackened and finally stopped altogether.

Not long after it ended, stars appeared to look down upon him, and an unseen nightbird sent him a shrill message he didn't understand.

It was, he estimated the following night, nearly midnight, judging by the position of the polestar, when he caught sight of a light glowing on the distant horizon ahead of him.

He was able to make out, with the help of the single light in the distance, the hulking shapes of buildings sprawled like lurking wooden beasts on both sides of the light.

Catoosa.

Between him and the town was the Verdigris River. As he came closer to it, he saw the moon drowning in its silvery water.

He decided not to ford the river until morning. He glanced at the light in the distance and wondered what it illuminated. Probably not a saloon because selling spirits in the territory was illegal. A private home? Did the light gleam on a woman getting ready for bed, her breasts rising provocatively as she raised her arms to unpin her pile of tawny hair?

He looked around him after halting his horse. There. A little to the north. A hummock. He rode over to it, got out of the saddle, and decided it would do.

He led his horse down to the river, and as it drank, so did he, kneeling on the riverbank and cupping water in his hands. Then he led the horse back to the western side of the hummock, which cast a deep shadow because of the half-moon, and stripped his gear from it. He spread his saddle blanket on the grass to dry and then used grass to rub his dun down. He cross-hobbled the animal, which dropped its head to graze, and then he lay down in the hummock's deep shadow where he was almost invisible and, using his saddle for a pillow, wrapped the blanket he had taken from his bedroll around him and let himself slip quickly into sleep and an arousing dream in which the imaginary woman in the lighted building in Catoosa bared her body and beckoned to him.

The day was already hours old when Cimarron awoke the next morning. He stretched, threw off his blanket, and

21

got up. With his eyes on Catoosa in the distance, he began to undress. He carried his clothes down to the river and washed them; then, after walking into the river, he washed himself.

Later, he sat naked on the soft early-summer grass, his clothes spread out on it beside him, as the sun rose higher in the sky and his horse lay down on the ground and began to roll.

The sun quickly dried his dripping body, and when it had also dried his clothes, he dressed, got his dun ready to move out, and stepped into the saddle.

He forded the Verdigris and walked his horse toward Catoosa, which was, he could now see, bordered on the north by a wide creek. Its builings were plain and many of them were unpainted. Most were one story. Some had a second story. A few were rather elaborately false-fronted. There was, he found as he rode into the town and along its dusty main street, no boardwalk.

There was a store that sold general merchandise and another that advertised itself by means of a chalked sign, as a source of PROVISIONS. Next to it was a building that looked like a saloon but whose sign read: DEVINE'S PLACE. No hotel, as far as he could see. Scattered on the fringes of the business district were individual houses, some of them not much more than hovels, but a few had white picket fences surrounding their small lawns.

He dismounted in front of a building that bore the word RESTAURANT painted on its window.

He wrapped his reins around the hitch rail in front of the restaurant and went inside. He sat down at a table halfway between the outer door and an inner one that led, he supposed, to a kitchen in the rear of the building. He sat with his back to the wall, positioning himself so that he had a clear view of both doors.

A man lounging at one of the tables on the other side of the room was reading a newspaper. He had looked up when Cimarron entered the room and nodded a wordless greeting.

The rear door opened and a gaunt woman with gray hair and a grim expression came through it. When she saw Cimarron, she strode over to him and asked, "What'll it be?"

22

"What've you got?"

"Nothing fancy."

"I could eat a rare steak or two. Some potatoes—fried or boiled'll be fine. Some bread and some butter if you've got any."

The woman left the table and disappeared through the rear door. When she returned some time later, she was carrying a huge platter which, when she set it down in front of him, Cimarron discovered contained everything he had ordered. The potatoes were boiled. The two steaks bled.

"I could do with some coffee to wash all this down with," he said to the woman.

"That'll be one-fifty," she said, and held out her hand.

Cimarron rummaged about in a pocket of his jeans and came up with the money, which he handed to the woman. "I really didn't plan to pick up this plate and make a run for it."

"I've known men to do as much," the woman said bluntly, and walked away after tucking the money Cimarron had given her into the pocket of the greasy apron she was wearing.

He had finished eating his first steak and was beginning to devour his second when she returned with a cracked china cup and a coffeepot. She put down the cup, filled it, and then placed the pot on the table. "You want seconds on the coffee, you're welcome. There's no extra charge." And then she was gone again.

The man with the newspaper coughed.

Cimarron emptied the cup of the lukewarm coffee it contained and then used a folded piece of bread that he had liberally buttered to mop up the juices that had leaked from his steaks.

His mouth was full of bread when the man seated across the room put down his newspaper and got up. He came over to Cimarron's table and said, "You're new in town."

"Brand new. Just got in."

"Planning on staying?"

"You keeping count of the citizens in Catoosa?"

Unruffled, the man said, "Just making conversation.

23

Men come. They go. This here's a shifty sort of town. In more ways than one."

"Know it well, do you?" Cimarron refilled his cup.

"Lived here quite a spell."

"Know a man by the name of Archie Kane?"

"Kane." The man scratched his head. "Don't think I do. Don't sound familiar, that name." He frowned. "Miz Perkins!" he bellowed.

When the aproned woman appeared from behind the rear door, the man asked, "You know anybody name of Archie Kane?"

"I don't know most of my customers' names," Mrs. Perkins snapped. "I just feed 'em and collect what they owe me. I mind my own business and see to it that they mind theirs." She vanished.

The man standing beside Cimarron's table said, "Try asking at Devine's Place. That's sort of the social center of this town for the men who live around here. They got pool tables. Card games. Like that." He winked at Cimarron. "And in back they got a special room where they sell the ardent. They close that room up real fast and tight if one of them deputy marshals happens to ride into town, which they don't do very often, which makes most people in this kind of town glad."

"Much obliged," Cimarron said. "I reckon I'll mosey on down to Devine's and have myself a look around."

"They've taken to watering the whiskey there," the man remarked mournfully. "It's hard to prove it, but I've no doubt they do on account of it's been costing me close to a mint lately to get good and drunk down there."

When Cimarron made no comment, the man ambled out of the restaurant.

Cimarron rose and followed him outside. He stood under the overhang for several minutes, scanning the street in both directions, noting the locations of various business establishments and which windows on the second stories of the buildings were closed and which were open.

A wagon, its driver yawning, rolled down the dirt street, turned a corner, and disappeared. A lone rider followed in its wake, dismounted, and went into the tin shop across the street.

Cimarron freed his horse and walked it toward Devine's Place.

When he reached his destination, he tethered the dun to the hitch rail outside and went into the building. He stood just inside the door for a moment until his eyes became accustomed to the poorly lighted and smoky interior.

There were several men seated at a table in one corner of the room playing cards. Another man was idly shooting pool by himself at one of the tables that lined one wall. The click of ball against ball was the only sound in the room, with the exception of an occasional grunted remark from one of the card players.

Cimarron glanced at them. A mix of cowboys and townsmen, he decided, judging by their clothes. The pool player, dressed in black from his derby hat to his patent-leather shoes, might have been mistaken for a minister except for the flint in his sharp eyes.

The floor beneath Cimarron's boots was sawdust-strewn and it was pocked here and there with tobacco wads and stained with tobacco juice. There wasn't a spittoon in the place.

A card player cursed and threw down his cards. He left the table, crossed the room, and angrily removed a cue from the wall rack.

Cimarron decided not to question that particular man about Archie Kane. At least, not right away. He was clearly a man whose anger was seeking a target. Cimarron decided to let him vent it in a game of pool.

He walked over to the card players and saw that a poker game was in progress.

One of the players looked up at him, a thin cigar dangling from a corner of his mouth.

" 'Morning," Cimarron greeted him.

The man looked down at his cards.

"I've been told that a man can buy himself a drink here."

When no one responded to his remark, Cimarron said, "A man as thirsty as I happen to be at the moment's been known to pay a premium price for a drink."

The man with the cigar looked up again and studied

25

Cimarron, who stood with his hands hooked in his cartridge belt.

"Who're you?" he finally asked, his cigar bobbing between his lips.

"A stranger passing through town is all. A thirsty stranger."

One of the men at the table swung around in his chair and stared up at Cimarron for a moment. "It's against the law to sell spirits in the territory."

"So I've heard tell. I'm out looking to break that particular law just about as fast as I can, and I sure would appreciate it if you gentlemen would point me the way to the ardent."

The man with the cigar said, "The man at the pool table over there." He pointed. "His name's Devine. He owns this place."

Cimarron turned and headed for the pool table.

"Lost everything but my shirt," the man who had deserted the card game was complaining to Devine as Cimarron reached the table. "Would've lost that too if I hadn't quit when I did."

"The game's a square one," Devine commented, and sent a ball ricocheting off another one and both of them down into pockets.

"I ain't saying it was a crooked game. But it's nigh on to uncanny how that man Brewster's luck runs. He raked in almost every pot."

Cimarron said, "I could use a drink."

Devine cooly pocketed another ball before looking up at him. "We don't sell drinks here."

"But you do in your back room," Cimarron said quietly.

Devine's eyes narrowed, studying Cimarron. And then, "Come on."

Cimarron followed him to a door in the rear wall which Devine unlocked. Cimarron stepped into a small room which had a bar that was formed by a raw wooden plank laid across two barrels. Behind it was a narrow shelf on which no more than half a dozen bottles rested.

"What'll you have?" Devine asked.

"Whiskey."

When Devine produced a bottle and glass, Cimarron

poured himself a drink and promptly downed it, realizing as he did so that the man he had spoken to in the restaurant had been right. The whiskey had been watered.

"I'm looking," he said as he refilled his glass, "for a man named Archie Kane."

Devine shook his head. "Ask Bill Boynton. He knows everybody in town. Even those that are just passing through. He might know the whereabouts of your man if he's here in Catoosa."

"Who's Boynton and where'll I find him?"

"He comes in here now and then. He's a heavy drinker. You're bound to run into him if you're around here much. Want another one?"

Cimarron shook his head.

"Two bits."

Cimarron paid and returned to the larger room, where he stood behind one of the poker players and watched the progress of the game. The man who had complained earlier had been right, he noted. One man seemed to be doing most of the winning, and when that man looked up and invited him to join the game, Cimarron did.

"We have a twenty-dollar limit," the man declared as Cimarron sat down at the table. "Hope that's not too rich for your blood. By the way, my name's Brewster."

When Cimarron said nothing, Brewster continued, "We're playing with a fifty-three-card deck." He began to deal the cards. "The deck includes an imperial trump, which can be played as an ace. Maybe you'll get a chance to play it that way."

"Be nice if I did, now wouldn't it?" Cimarron picked up his cards. "What's the top hand in this game? I've found it varies from place to place, so I'd just like to make certain. Is it a straight flush here like in some other places I've been?"

"No," said one of the other two players. "Not in this game. Four aces will beat a straight flush. But four kings and an ace will beat even that."

As the game progressed, Cimarron found himself with two pair. He lost to Brewster. Later, he lost again to Brewster, who beat his pat flush with a full house.

A few minutes later, Brewster called him.

Cimarron looked at the cards in his hand, remembering

27

what the man had told him about the top hand in this particular game. The man had said, he recalled, that four aces could be beaten only by four kings and an ace. Well, he thought, it looks like I've caught the wind in my hat. He held four aces, so he knew that no one else could be holding an ace. He placed his cards on the table.

Brewster slapped down four kings. And then the imperial trump.

Cimarron groaned. He had completely forgotten about the fifty-third card in the deck, which could be played as an ace.

After Brewster had collected his winnings and the game resumed, Cimarron began to surreptitiously examine the cards as they passed through his hands. He could detect no carefully placed watermarks on any of them. He found no rounded corners and no shaved cards. But as he ran the tips of his fingers over the backs of the cards he was holding, he detected a series of bumps on their surfaces. The pattern of bumps varied from card to card. He looked up at Brewster and watched the man's fingers carefully caressing the backs of the cards as he dealt them.

"Brewster," he said in a low voice. "I'm taking back the money I lost to you."

"Like hell you are!" Brewster snarled.

"Like hell I am," Cimarron countered. "You've been cheating, Brewster. You used a card pricker on this deck."

The other two players at the table looked at Cimarron in surprise.

"Run your fingers along the backs of your cards," he told them. "You'll feel the bumps Brewster's card pricker's raised on them so that he could tell the value of each card as it passed through his hands."

As the other two men began to examine their cards, Cimarron said, "I'll take back what I lost now, Brewster, and then I'll be leaving." He reached out toward the pile of money lying on the table in front of Brewster.

But before he could touch it, Brewster pulled a Smith & Wesson .32 from his waistband and aimed it at Cimarron.

"Get out of here!" he barked at Cimarron.

One of the players grunted. "What the man said is true, Brewster. You've been cheating all along!"

"Devine!" Brewster yelled.

When Devine appeared from the back room, Brewster said, "Get their guns."

Devine hurried over to the table and took the guns the two players quickly handed him. He turned to Cimarron.

Cimarron slowly unholstered his Colt and handed it over.

"Now step away from the table," Brewster ordered him. "Hands up high."

Cimarron stood up, raised his hands, and stepped back. He fell over his chair—deliberately. At almost the instant he hit the floor, he pulled his bowie knife from his boot and came up fast.

Brewster fired his belly gun at him and missed.

Cimarron came in low and fast and brought his bowie down hard as Brewster fired at him a second time, hitting the wall behind Cimarron.

The blade of Cimarron's bowie hit into the back of Brewster's right hand, knocking the gun from it which fell to the floor. The force of Cimarron's action brought Brewster's hand down. It hit the table. The knife went through it and pinned Brewster's hand to the table.

Brewster screamed.

Cimarron, with a single sharp tug, pulled his bowie free and quickly placed its bloody blade against Brewster's throat.

"Devine," he said, "don't use any of those guns you're holding. Or I'll slit the throat of your partner here. How much of a share of his winnings do you get?"

Devine remained silent.

"I asked you a question, Devine." Cimarron pressed the bowie against Brewster's throat.

"Tell him!" Brewster screeched as the cut Cimarron had made in the flesh of his throat began to bleed. "Devine, tell him, for Christ's sake!"

"Thirty percent," Devine muttered.

Cimarron held out his left hand. "I'll take back my six-gun, Devine."

When Devine handed it to him, he said to Brewster, "I'd hoped to be able to settle this matter in a more peaceable manner, but you thought you could take me. That was your second mistake. Your first was thinking you could cheat me and get away with it."

He withdrew his knife from Brewster's throat, wiped its bloody blade on his jeans, and thrust it into his boot.

With his cocked Colt in his right hand, he reached out with his left and picked up twenty-one dollars, the amount he had lost in the game, from the pile of bills and coins lying on the table in front of Brewster. He backed toward the door, the four men in the room watching his retreat, none of them moving.

As he went through the door, he saw Brewster's eyes begin to fill with tears and his lips start to tremble as he stared down at his savaged right hand.

3

Cimarron quickly crossed the street.

He took up a position behind a wooden pillar supporting an overhang in front of a building that housed a feed store. His cocked revolver remained in his hand.

He waited, his eyes on the door of Devine's Place.

Devine came to the door and peered out. When he spotted Cimarron standing across the street, he ducked back inside, closing the door behind him.

Cimarron continued to wait, noting the passageway that ran between Devine's Place and the building next to it. Shadows filled it.

But he was able to make out, a few minutes later, the figures of Devine and Brewster heading at right angles across the end of the passageway in the rear of the buildings. Brewster was hunched over, gripping his right wrist with his left hand. Devine walked stolidly beside him.

The two men vanished behind the adjacent building.

Cimarron eased the hammer of his Colt back into place and then turned and went into the feed store.

"Yes, sir?"

To the man behind the counter, Cimarron said, "I'd like to buy some grain. An even mix of oats and barley. About a pound's worth."

"Certainly, sir."

Cimarron watched the clerk scoop the oats and barley from two wooden bins and pour them into a cloth sack. After weighing the sack on his metal scale, he handed it to Cimarron, who paid for it and said, "I'm looking for a man named Archie Kane. You happen to know him by any chance?"

"No, I don't."

"How about a man named Bill Boynton?"

"He lives just outside of town. He's been letting his place go to rack and ruin lately. He doesn't do much farming these days. He drinks instead."

"Where's his place located exactly?"

"South of town. A little to the east near the river. He's got good bottomland, for all the good it's doing him these days. This Archie Kane fellow you're hunting. I can tell you something about him too."

"Thought you said you didn't know him."

"That's right, I did. But I can tell you he's no stockman from around here. If he was, he'd have been in here to buy grain. I'd have got to know him. I'll tell you something else about him too."

"What might that be?"

"He's not a resident of Catoosa. Most of us know everybody in town. Catoosa's not that big. This Kane fellow's a drifter, an in-and-outer like a lot of others who are here today and gone tomorrow."

"Much obliged."

Outside again, Cimarron crossed the street, stowed the sack he was carrying in his saddlebag, and freed his horse. Minutes later, Catoosa was behind him as he rode south, scanning the countryside, searching for Boynton's home.

He found it a little while later and rode east toward it. Dismounting in front of the house, he noted the frayed curtains in the windows, the almost-nonexistent woodpile beneath the lean-to that stood beside the house, and the open front door.

Now he too knew something about Boynton as the grain merchant evidently did. He knew that Boynton was careless.

He went up to the open door and knocked on it.

He obtained no response.

"Boynton!" he called out.

Silence.

He stepped inside and looked around the untidy parlor he found beyond the door. No Boynton. He moved on into the kitchen at the rear of the house. It was empty.

Dirty dishes littered the table that stood in the middle of the room.

He went out the back door and looked around. He was alone except for a single cow in a distant pasture and several scrawny Rhode Island Reds that were scratching at the ground and ignoring him.

He walked around the house and then climbed back into the saddle and headed back to Catoosa. He decided to head for Devine's Place. Maybe Boynton would show up there. Devine had said that Boynton spent a lot of time at his place and the grain merchant had commented on Boynton's drinking. Then Devine's Place was as likely a spot to find the man as any other. It was also, Cimarron knew, a likely place to find trouble, considering what had recently happened to him there.

But what could Brewster do to him? Nothing much, he decided. Not with his right hand in the shape it now was. And Devine didn't look like much of a fighter. He was, Cimarron believed, more of a carrion eater than a killer. He was the kind of man who'd move in after somebody else had done all the dirty work.

Still, it wouldn't do to take any chances. But then he seldom did, under any circumstances. Not unless the odds were decidedly in his favor.

He never got back to Devine's Place.

When he first saw her, she was standing in front of the restaurant and he had slowed his horse even before she smiled at him. Her smile made him halt the dun and sit his saddle, smiling back at her.

Not bad, he thought. Pretty good, in fact. She was a bit faded, though, and her eyes looked weary. She was about thirty, give or take a year or two. Yellow hair and big brown eyes. Big-bosomed, Cimarron noted, his smile widening, and even bigger-hipped. A woman to comfort a man if he ever saw one. A woman to sink down into and let her fold her ampleness all around him while he went at it with her.

She was wearing a gray skirt and high button patent-leather shoes. Above her skirt and over her breasts, she wore a simple white blouse with a black ribbon threaded through the eyelets encircling her neck.

"I know you," she said to him, and Cimarron got out

33

of the saddle and led his horse over to where she stood. "You're a very dangerous man."

"Now, how would you know me?" he asked, touching the brim of his hat to her. "Or know—believe—that I'm a dangerous man."

"Well, I can usually tell about a man. But this time I happen to have been advised of that fact when you were described to me. Nearly everyone in town has heard by now about what you did to that tinhorn gambler in Devine's Place."

"I'm sorry to hear that, on account of it might make some folks think unkindly of me."

"I don't think at all unkindly of you."

"How do you think about me?"

"I am far too modest to answer that question."

"Are you, now? Is that a fact? I admire modesty in a woman just so long as she doesn't carry it too far and let it get in the way of her having some enjoyment in this vale of tears we're all confined in."

"Oh, I assure you that I find my share of enjoyment. I imagine you do too."

"From time to time, I do, yes. Especially when I meet up with a woman such as yourself. It's a pure pleasure just to look at you, I don't mind saying."

"My, I'm surprised that a man like you, who has a bowie knife in his boot and knows how to use it, can talk so pretty."

"I'm called Cimarron."

"Ella. Ella Bantry."

"Glad to know you, Miss Bantry. Is it *Miss* Bantry?"

"It is."

"And you live here in Catoosa?"

"I do."

"Catoosa—that is to say the men in it—ought to consider themselves most fortunate."

Ella smiled her appreciation of Cimarron's remark and then waved one hand in front of her face to fan it. "My, it is such a terribly hot day, isn't it? It just wrings a body bone dry."

"I can think of a cure for that condition. Let's you and me go inside Mrs. Perkins' establishment here. We'll see if

34

she has some lemonade I can buy you." He wrapped the dun's reins around the hitch rail in front of the restaurant.

"I have an even better idea, Cimarron."

"You have?" He met her gaze, hoping.

"We'll go to my place. I haven't any lemonade, but water will do just as well for me. You'll want something stronger, I expect, and I can supply it."

"You look to me like a woman who can supply most of what a man might be needing."

Another smile, this time impish.

"Which way to your place?"

Ella pointed north and as they started out in that direction, she took Cimarron's arm.

"It sure is nice to meet somebody friendly after what happened to me in Devine's Place," he told her sincerely.

"I'm a very friendly person."

"I can see that." Cimarron could also see that there were two women across the street whispering together, their disapproving eyes on Ella Bantry. As he walked on with Ella, they passed several men, each of whom spoke to her, all of them using her first name just as she called them by their first names.

It added up, Cimarron thought, and the sum equaled his high hopes for this chance encounter, hopes that had just been reinforced because at least two women of the town clearly disapproved of Ella Bantry and several men clearly more than merely approved of her, if one were to judge by the friendly—even intimate—greetings they had given her. A man didn't have to be a scholar to draw a solid conclusion from those few facts, he was convinced.

"Cimarron, will you excuse me for just a moment?"

He watched Ella cross the street to speak with a raw-boned man who was leaning against a wooden water trough and who had been watching them, his booted ankles crossed, his hams of hands folded across his thick chest.

The conversation between Ella and the man at the water trough was brief, and when she returned and took Cimarron's arm again, the rawboned man turned and headed south.

"Friend of yours?" Cimarron inquired.

"Who? Oh, you mean Johnny Adams. No, not really. I

35

need some wood chopped and Johnny has obliged me in the past."

"You seem to know most of the men in town."

"I told you I'm a very friendly person."

"I am too," Cimarron assured her, and felt himself stiffening as a result of the overwhelming friendliness he was feeling for Ella Bantry.

"Here we are," she declared a moment later, stopping in front of a one-story clapboard house that stood some distance away from the commercial buildings of Catoosa.

As she opened her front door, Cimarron commented, "Seems no one in Catoosa or near it bothers to lock their doors. The people around here must be mighty trusting of one another."

"Who else's door have you found to be unlocked?"

"Man named Boynton. Paid him a visit just before I met you but he wasn't home to be visited."

"You're a friend of Billy's?" Ella asked as she led Cimarron into the parlor and proceeded to draw the window blinds.

"Nope. But I've been told he might know the whereabouts of a man I'm looking for. A man named Archie Kane."

"I know Archie. He's visited me on several occasions, but I haven't seen him during the past few days. Would you like some whiskey?"

Cimarron nodded, and as Ella started toward the rear of the house, he asked, "Where does he stay when he's in town—Kane, I mean?"

"I really couldn't say." And then Ella was gone.

Cimarron looked around the parlor. Antimacassars on the backs of overstuffed chairs and an equally overstuffed sofa with its share of antimacassars, all of which showed traces of hair pomade.

Which women didn't use as a rule, Cimarron thought happily.

A cactus growing in a clay pot on the windowsill. An empty fireplace flanked by shiny brass andirons. China figurines neatly arranged on a square table—puppies, kittens, geese, a squirrel.

Definitely a woman's room and one in which male

36

guests had been entertained. Entertained? A ghost of a grin appeared on Cimarron's face and was quickly gone.

Ella reappeared, a glass half-full of whiskey in her hand. "I didn't add any water. Is that all right?"

"If you had added some, I'd be inclined to say you'd make out well in the back room of Devine's Place."

"I beg your pardon?"

"It's not important. Just a stray thought I should have kept corralled." He accepted the glass she held out to him. "You're not having any?"

"Any what?" she asked coquettishly.

He set the glass down in the midst of the figurines and placed his hands gently on her shoulders.

She stood with her hands neatly clasped in front of her and looked up at him.

He stepped closer to her and felt his hardness touch her clasped hands.

She continued to stare up at him. Her hands didn't move.

He bent down and covered her lips with his. He promptly parted his lips and thrust his tongue against her teeth, which opened. He began to probe within her mouth as his arms enfolded her.

When their kiss ended, Ella drew a deep breath and said, "Are you always—so ready?" She pressed her still-clasped hands teasingly against his erection and then unfolded them and wrapped them around his waist.

"A woman like you has a way of readying any man who's not dead or dying."

Ella withdrew from him, picked up his glass, and handed it to him.

He took it from her, although whiskey was the last thing in the world he wanted at the moment.

"I'm rather expensive," she said.

"I can pay—if your price's not too steep. How much?"

"Ten dollars."

"Haven't run into a bargain like you in too long a time." He raised his glass to her and then drank from it.

Ella went to one of the windows and peeped around the edge of the blind.

"You afraid somebody might be spying on us?" Cimarron asked her.

"What?" She turned back to him, her hands nervously smoothing her skirt. "Oh, no, I'm not afraid of that. I just wanted to make sure that Johnny Adams wasn't coming. We don't want to be interrupted, do we?"

"Try locking the door so's we won't be." Cimarron emptied his glass and set it down again. "Honey, I'm ready if you are."

Ella left the window and led him out of the parlor, down a short hall, and into a bedroom where the shades were also drawn.

He smelled lilac perfume in the room.

She held out her hand to him.

He was about to take it in his own when he saw the cool glint in her eyes and realized what her gesture meant. He reached into the pocket of his jeans, pulled out some folded bills, peeled off a ten, and handed it to her.

As she lifted her skirt and tucked the money into her garter, he realized that she didn't intend to undress, at least not completely. He suppressed a sigh and went over and sat down on the bed. He unbuckled his gun rig and placed it on the floor beside the bed before lying down on his back and spreading his legs.

Ella came over to the bed, climbed up on it, and knelt between his legs. She began to unbutton his jeans.

"Oh, my," she whispered as she freed him and he snapped erect. "I've known some big men in my time, but I do believe without a doubt that you are the biggest I've ever met."

"Seems like it just grew a whole lot faster than all the rest of me did."

"What does it like best?"

"Best? Well, now, I don't think it has a particular preference. It likes just about anything at all. To be petted, stroked . . ." He raised a hand and touched her lips with his index finger. "It sure does like to be tasted. It likes finding its way into all sorts of places."

Ella slid her warm hand along the length of him and he suppressed the desire to seize her, throw her down on her back, and plunge into her. But no. Let her take her time. He'd lie back and enjoy her teasing for a time; that would make the climax of their encounter all the better when it finally arrived.

She tightened her grip on him and then lowered her head. Her lips parted and her tongue flicked out.

Cimarron felt its warmth and wetness, and his pelvis involuntarily arched upward, part of him disappearing inside her mouth.

"Good?" she asked a moment later, straightening up but still holding him tightly in one firm hand.

"That way's just fine with me if it suits you," he responded. "Just fine," he repeated a moment later as she once again bent down and took him in her mouth and simultaneously began to manipulate him with her right hand.

"Don't use your hand," he whispered huskily. "Just use your—" He moaned as she withdrew her hand and lowered her head even farther, obeying his order.

Her head began to bob up and down, slowly at first and them more rapidly.

Cimarron moaned again, his hands clenched at his sides, his knees rising.

Suddenly she released him and almost leaped from the bed.

He opened his eyes, which he had closed as she began to service him. "Hey!" he cried. "What—"

"The door. I forgot to lock it."

As she hurried from the room, Cimarron sighed, looking down at his wet erection, willing Ella to return quickly and finish what she had so professionally started.

When several minutes had passed and she still had not returned, he called her name. She didn't respond. He called her name a second time, staring in disgust at his wilting flesh.

He got up from the bed, and after tucking himself back into his jeans and then buttoning them, he went to the door of the room and peered down the hall. Ella was nowhere to be seen. Nor could he hear her moving about anywhere in the house.

What, he wondered, had happened? She had seemed to be enjoying herself with him. Then, why had she disappeared?

A frown appeared on his face.

Had something happened to her? He strode down the hall. As he entered the parlor, he saw her. She was standing stiffly on the far side of the room, arms rigid at her sides, an unreadable expression on her face as she stared at him.

He took a step toward her. "Honey, what's wrong? Why'd you go and run off from me like that?"

He saw her eyes flicker and then felt the blow delivered by someone who had come up behind him. It struck at the base of his neck, knocking him off balance. He staggered forward, collided with the table, and overturned it, sending the china figurines that had been on it crashing to the floor, where most of them shattered.

Before he could regain his balance, he heard the clink of spurs behind him. The second blow given him by his unseen attacker caught him in the small of his back, and as pain erupted within him, he felt an urgent need to urinate.

He tripped over the fallen table and went down, his knees cracking against the bare wooden floor. As he tried to rise, a booted foot slammed against his ribs and sent him careening to one side. He hit the wall hard.

Blinking away the gray fog that was swirling around him, he saw the rawboned man standing above him, his hands fisted, his body bent. He knew the man. He had seen him somewhere. Where? And then he remembered. The man standing so menacingly over him was the man Ella had crossed the street to speak to on the way to the house. His name? It came to him. Johnny Adams, that was it. Adams was supposed to chop some wood for Ella. Then, why the hell, Cimarron thought, doesn't he try chopping wood instead of chopping me?

As Adams' right fist shot downward toward his face, Cimarron rolled out of its path. Then he was up on his feet and grabbing for Adams who suddenly brought up one knee and rammed it into Cimarron's groin.

Cimarron doubled over in pain, gasping and clutching his genitals, unable to breathe, although his mouth was wide open and he was desperately trying to suck air into his lungs.

He quickly backed away from Adams, almost hopping, playing for time until he could breathe normally again.

Adams sprang toward him.

But to Cimarron, his opponent seemed to be moving in

slow motion. The smile on Adams' face mocked him, and Cimarron wanted to reach out and smash that smile, smash it again and again until it was only an ugly memory in the mass of torn and ravaged flesh that was all he had left of Adams' features.

Cimarron released his hold on his genitals, and as Adams swung a furious right, he ducked, came in under it, and landed a crushing left against Adams' jaw. Adams took the blow as if it had been merely a slap. He threw a fast left that struck Cimarron's chest and then a faster right that Cimarron fended off with a raised left forearm.

He connected with an uppercut to Adams' jaw and then, sidestepping quickly, threw a left cross that bounced off Adams' shoulder.

As Adams pursued him, Cimarron continued to side-step, moving in a circle, fists raised, body in a crouching position. He watched carefully for an opening, but Adams gave him none.

Then, a moment later, Cimarron saw his chance as Adams lunged at him. He stepped forward to meet the man, slamming both of his fists against Adams' shoulders and then grabbing his shirt with both hands. As Adams was knocked backward by the maneuver, Cimarron moved his left leg forward and then, carefully to maintain his balance, raised his right leg and swung it in an arc between his left and Adams' right leg.

Still gripping Adams' shirt with both hands, he brought his right leg back along the arc it had traveled and rammed it behind Adams' right knee. At the same instant, he shoved hard with both hands and Adams fell backward and hit the floor.

Cimarron dropped down upon him and used both fists, one after the other, on the man's face and head as he straddled him.

Something moved on his right. From the corner of his eye, he saw Ella hurrying toward the fireplace.

Adams reached up and punched him in the throat. Cimarron gagged.

Then Adams pushed Cimarron backward and slid out from beneath him, but before he could get to his feet, Cimarron seized him by the throat and slammed the back of his head against the wooden floor several times.

41

Adams' eyes closed as he lost consciousness. His body went limp.

Cimarron, massaging his aching throat, started to rise.

But before he could get to his feet, he saw Ella moving swiftly in his direction, the brass andiron she had taken from in front of the fireplace held high above her head in both hands. As the andiron came flying down toward him, Cimarron threw up his right arm. He succeeded in partially deflecting the blow, but the andiron nevertheless grazed the side of his head, sending pain skyrocketing through his skull and instantly and totally ending his awareness of the world around him.

The blackness in which he drifted shifted and then seemed to roil like water rushing down a dry wash after a cloudburst. It softened and became gray—the faint light that preceded a clear dawn.

Pain.

In his body. Mostly in his head. The pain was a scream that almost deafened him as he opened his eyes, to find himself lying facedown on grass. He remained motionless for a moment and then tried to raise his head. The pain splintered, sending shards of itself throughout his skull. He forced himself to remain still, his head hanging down, his hair falling in front of his face as he stared down at the ground without seeing it.

And then he turned and sat down, drawing his knees up and folding his arms on them. He let his forehead rest on his folded arms.

After some time had passed, he gingerly raised his head. He lifted one hand and touched the point on the side of his head where the pain lived.

Blood.

He stared at his hand and at the blood on it before angrily wiping his hand on his jeans. He untied his bandanna and pressed it against the wound on the side of his head.

He looked up at the stars in the night sky and then around him. He was alone out in the open, no landmark that he could recognize anywhere near him. Only the open land, sprinkled here and there with a few tall trees as alone as he was visible.

Adams, he thought. Ella Bantry.

She had set him up for Adams, he realized. He reached into the pocket of his jeans. As he had suspected, his money was gone.

Well, he would damn well get it back.

He slowly got to his feet, looked around, and saw his slouch hat and gun rig lying on the ground. He bent over and picked them up. He almost fell over while doing so because of the dizziness that washed over him, sending the world into a giddy whirl.

He straightened and clapped his hat on his head.

After strapping on his cartridge belt, he adjusted it until it hung low and easy on his hips. Then he unholstered his Colt and checked its cylinder. No shells had been removed from it. Five of its six chambers were loaded. The hammer rested on the empty chamber. He turned the cylinder so that there was a bullet beneath the hammer and then slid the .45 back into its leather.

He began walking west, hoping he was headed in the right direction.

He had walked for some time and was on the verge of turning back when he made out a light up ahead of him. A light that burned in one of Catoosa's buildings.

A few minutes later, walking slowly, he entered the town and headed for the house where Ella Bantry lived— and worked in her opportunistic way, he thought, on men like himself.

When he reached the house, he tried the front door and found it locked. Maybe the back door would be open. To hell with the back door, he thought, and raised his right foot to send his boot banging up against the locked door as he simultaneously drew his .45.

Wood splintered and the door burst open.

From the rear of the house came the startled cry of a woman.

Cimarron strode through the dark parlor and down the hall. Suddenly a sliver of light slid out from beneath the bedroom door.

He threw open the door and found Ella sitting up in bed, a sheet drawn up to her chin. Beside her, Adams was reaching for his six-gun, which rested on a bedside table beside a lighted lamp.

"Hold it, Adams!" Cimarron said sharply, and Adams quickly withdrew his reaching hand.

"Don't shoot me!" Adams muttered, sleep slowing his voice.

"I don't intend to shoot you. I downed you before. Our score's settled—except for the money you stole from me. I want it."

"I don't have it!" Adams declared, his eyes wide as he stared at Cimarron. "Honest, I don't."

"You got it?" Cimarron asked Ella.

She shook her head.

"Who has it, then?"

Adams was silent. So was Ella.

Cimarron put a bullet in the wall behind them.

"Brewster!" Adams cried shrilly.

"How the hell does Brewster figure in all of this?" Cimarron asked angrily.

"Ella works for him," Adams replied. "She's been his whore for a year now. He told her what you did to him. He described you to her. He told her to be on the lookout for you. I was supposed to keep my eye on her to see if she connected with you; when she told me she had, I told Brewster and he told me to take care of you. Sort of pay you back for what you did to him. When I came to before, I hauled you out of town and chucked you and your belongings like Brewster told me to do. He figured you wouldn't come back—that you'd've learned your lesson."

"I never was much of a scholar." Cimarron glanced at Ella, who was staring sullenly at him, and then back at Adams. "She charging you ten dollars? Or does overnight cost more?"

"Brewster turned her over to me for the night," Adams said, his tone as sullen as Ella's expression. "As a sort of reward for taking care of you."

"For *trying* to take care of me." Cimarron shifted his stance slightly. "Now, then," he said, trying to ignore the pain thudding in his head. "We three are going to pay Brewster a late-night visit. But first"—he turned to Ella—"I want my ten dollars back, seeing as how I never got from you what I paid for."

"Brewster has it," Ella said dully. "I turn all my earnings over to him."

"Then let's go see him," Cimarron said.

Ella reached for her clothes, which were draped over a chair near the bed, as Adams reached for his pants, which lay in a heap with his other clothes on the floor.

When they were both dressed, Cimarron gestured, and as they left the bedroom, he followed them out into the hall and then out of the house.

As he walked behind them through the business district, he noticed with relief that his horse was still tethered outside the restaurant where he had left it.

They went down an alley that led to a wooden shack on the western edge of town.

"Knock," Cimarron ordered Ella.

She did, and at the same time called out, "Carl! It's me, Ella. Open up!"

Brewster's muffled voice came from behind the closed door. "Get the hell away from here. It's the middle of the goddamn night!"

"Mr. Brewster!" Adams called out, shivering although the night was mild. "Ella and me, we got to talk to you, boss."

Curses from inside the shack.

And then the door swung open.

Brewster, wearing only long johns and a bandage on his right hand, stood, a white blur, blinking in the doorway. "You!" he exclaimed when he saw Cimarron standing behind Ella and Adams.

"Me," Cimarron said.

Once they were all inside the house, he ordered Brewster to light a lamp, which the man promptly did.

It gave little light because of its smoky glass globe, which looked to Cimarron as if it hadn't been cleaned in months.

"I came for my money, Brewster," he said, his voice low.

"What money?"

Ella said, "Carl, it won't do to try to lie to him. We had to tell him everything."

"That's right, boss," Adams said, his voice apologetic.

"Damn fools, both of you!" Brewster muttered.

"My money, Brewster," Cimarron said, brandishing his Colt. "I want it."

Grumbling, Brewster opened a drawer of a legless dresser at the rear of the room.

But when he turned away from it, he had no money in his hand. In his left hand was a Colt .44.

Cimarron fired before Brewster could pull the trigger of his revolver.

Brewster staggered forward, his hands trembling. He dropped the gun and began to fall. He reached out, his fingers finding Ella's arm. He brought her down with him.

She quickly scrambled to her feet.

"Jesus!" Adams murmured, awed. "Oh, Jesus Christ, you killed him, mister!"

"Did, didn't I?"

Cimarron crossed the room and took a wad of bills out of the open dresser drawer. He turned, his Colt trained on Adams and Ella, who stood side by side like obedient soldiers awaiting orders, and counted out the money they had taken from him, including the ten dollars he had earlier paid Ella.

"Score's settled now," he told them, looking down at the dead Brewster. "There's nothing more you two can do here. You might as well go on back and salvage what sleep you can out of what's left of the night."

"You're not going to kill us?" Adams asked, his voice cracking on the word "kill."

"Now, why would I want to go and do a thing like that? I told you, Adams, I beat the shit out of you, despite the dirty way you like to fight. So that makes you and me even." He glanced at Ella, who was staring at Brewster's bloody chest. "Honey, I think you just might have turned out to be the best whore I ever had. Pity I won't get to find out if my speculation's right or not."

Ella looked up at him and then down at the money he was holding in his left hand. Up at him again. A smile, very tentative, very uncertain. "Now that Carl's dead," she said softly, "the ten dollars I earn would be all mine to keep."

Cimarron nodded and gave her a rakish wink. "You're a real professional. A workingwoman through and through. But no, thanks just the same. Maybe some other time, when I'm so hard up I'd even take a chance on

46

risking my neck with the likes of you and your brass and-irons."

"You're gonna let us go now?" Adams asked hopefully.

"Git!"

When they both had fled, Cimarron looked down at Brewster and shook his head. "You should have quit after making your first two mistakes with me. Your third one was trying to throw down on me and just look at what it went and got you."

He left the shack and slipped like a shadow through the night until he reached his horse, which was standing in front of the restaurant. After releasing its reins, he stepped into the saddle and rode out of town, heading south.

4

Cimarron awoke at first light and lay on his back, staring up at the leaden sky.

Then he threw off his blanket, sat up, shook out his boots, and pulled them on. He reached for his hat, and pain flared in his head, reminding him of the night just ended. He let his hat lay where it was and got to his feet.

He went down to the stream where he had washed his wound hours earlier before bedding down for what remained of the night. He pulled his damp bandanna from the pocket of his jeans and dipped it in the stream as he had done upon arriving at the spot he had chosen to spend the night.

He winced as he wiped away dried blood, deliberately opening his wound to let the blood flow and cleanse it with the help of the water he had soaked up in his bandanna.

When he was satisfied that he had done all he could to help himself under the circumstances, he went back to where his dun stood beside a thicket of post oak and removed the sack of grain from his saddlebag. He fed the horse, the animal's teeth grazing his heavily callused hand as it ate the grain covering his palm.

When the horse had eaten the grain, Cimarron returned the empty sack to his saddlebag, made up his bedroll, and got the dun ready to ride out. He stuffed his wet bandanna into the crown of his hat to help cool his head as he rode beneath the rising sun, which would be, he suspected, as hot today as it had been the day before. He gingerly placed his hat on his head, tilting it at an odd angle so that it would not come into contact with the raw flesh of his head wound.

Less than ten minutes later, he sat his saddle in front of Boynton's house. He hallooed the house but received no answer.

"Were I to burn that house down," he said aloud, "it's likely that Boynton'd never miss it. Where the hell does the man go to roost?"

The troop of Rhode Island Reds, in ragged formation, scratched in the dirt for gravel as they marched erratically toward him. They reminded Cimarron of his earlier visit to Boynton's house. They reminded him of the cow he had seen in the pasture during that earlier visit.

He got out of the saddle and left his horse behind him as he rounded the house, scattering the chickens, which flapped, squalking, out of his path.

The cow was near the back door, he discovered, and when the animal saw him, it lowed and lumbered toward him.

He bent down and felt its bag. Full.

The cow lowed again and bumped against him.

"Now just you hold on a minute, old girl," he said, and looked around him.

A metal pail sat on the bench next to the back door. Cimarron went to it, and as he was about to pick it up, he smelled the stench coming from the residue of curdled milk that covered the pail's bottom.

"Boynton lives worse'n a blind pig," he muttered in disgust, and returned to the cow, dropping to his knees beside the animal.

He gripped one of the cow's udders in his right hand and angled it upward, lowering his head as he did so.

He opened his mouth to receive the warm white stream of milk he released from the udder. His aim was bad at first and more milk spattered his face than found its way into his mouth. But a few minutes later, his aim improved and he continued to drink his breakfast. When he had had enough, he continued to milk the cow to relieve her, deftly squeezing and jerking udders, two at a time now, and sending the milk splashing into the dirt as he damned Boynton, who clearly hadn't milked the animal for a day or more.

"There you go, old girl," he said when the cow's udders went dry. "Bet you feel a whole hundred percent better now. So do I, thanks to you."

He stood up, wiped his lips with the back of his hand, and stared at the chickens, which were busily scratching, heads up and then down, to find whatever treasures they might have unearthed, then up again as they continued to scratch.

He wondered if Boynton knew exactly how many chickens he owned. Would he miss one if it were to mysteriously disappear? Cimarron doubted it, but he nevertheless rejected the idea he had been considering and looked away from the chickens, scanning the countryside around him as he searched for some sign of Boynton.

He found none.

When his horse ambled into view around the corner of the house, he went over to it and was about to climb back into the saddle when he heard a muffled thud from inside the house. His right hand went to the butt of his .45.

He heard a moan that also had come from inside the house.

"Boynton!" he yelled. "You in there, Boynton?"

Another moan.

Cimarron went to the back door of the house, opened it, and stepped inside, his hand still on his six-gun.

He listened and heard someone shuffling about. He traced the sound to a door that opened off the hall. Drawing his Colt, he cautiously opened it.

An old man lay quivering on the floor beside the bed.

Cimarron watched as the man struggled to his feet, muttering incoherently as he did so.

"Boynton?"

The old man, clutching the edge of the bed for support, shook his gray hair and groaned. Then, cocking his head to one side, he said, "Who the hell might you be, mister?"

"Name's Cimarron. Came out here looking for you if you're Boynton."

"That's my name." Boynton swore. "I feel worse than Christ crucified and unable to die."

"What's the matter with you?" Cimarron asked, leathering his gun.

Boynton straightened and scratched his head. He

rubbed his reddened eyes and said, "Nothing a good stiff drink won't cure, at least temporarily." He tottered toward Cimarron, who stepped out of his way and then followed Boynton into the dirty kitchen.

He watched as Boynton searched the cupboards.

The old man was wearing bib overalls, scuffed boots, and a filthy flannel shirt.

Boynton found what he had been searching for behind a can of Arbuckle's coffee. He opened the whiskey bottle and took a deep drink.

"*Aahhh!*" he sighed as he sat down at the table and set the bottle on it. "Before long I won't be feeling so much like a hen that's been raped by a long line of roosters. Before long I'll be feeling as slick as a snake that's just shed it's skin." He took another long drink and then tossed his head to get his wispy hair out of his eyes.

The man's not seen a barber since before Methuselah was born, Cimarron thought. Hasn't touched soap and water for long before that. He could smell the man's sour stench. Trying to ignore it, he sat down at the table opposite Boynton.

"Drink?" Boynton offered him the bottle.

"No, thanks. I came here to find out if you know a man by the name of Archie Kane."

"Sure I know him. Know him fairly well, as a matter of fact."

"Where can I find him?"

"Why're you looking for him?"

"He's supposed to testify at a trial in Fort Smith."

"You're a lawman?"

"I am. A deputy marshal working out of Judge Parker's court."

"I was always a law-abiding man, son. But lately, if there was any law out here in this sinful Sodom to abide by, I'd've been arrested for being drunk and disorderly more times than a grown man can count."

"Where can I find Kane?"

Boynton waved a hand, nearly knocking over his bottle in the process. "Who the hell knows? The terrirory's got more nooks and crannies for a man to hide in than that new wire they're using now's got barbs."

"Kane's gone to ground, has he?"

"I didn't say that."

"Look, Boynton. I've got no time to make polite conversation with you. I've got to find Kane and take him back to Fort Smith. If you know where he is, I sure do wish you'd tell me so's I can get the hell out of here and leave you to the business of drinking yourself to death, since that's what you seem bound and determined to do."

"That's what I'm doing, all right. And it's all her fault, the bitch."

Boynton put the bottle to his lips and tilted it toward the ceiling.

"She left me," he said, whiskey trickling down his stubbled chin. "Her name was Margaret and she was a beauty in her prime. Good woman. Strong woman. Only, the two of us could never have any kids. Don't know why. It was hard on her at first when we found out. Hard on me too, were I to tell you the truth. But then time passed, as it has a way of doing, and we sort of got used to the way things were for us.

"In a funny kind of way, it brought us a lot closer together. But did I tell you? She left me, goddamn her to hell and the horny hands of Lucifer himself."

"About Archie Kane—"

"It wasn't right for her to go and do that to me. Not right atall." Boynton's body shuddered briefly. "Last year. That's when it happened. She'd been coughing up blood for a long time. She tried hard to hide it from me at first, but I noticed. She got pale and awful thin. Toward the end there, those coughing fits of hers used to rip into me the same way they were ripping her to pieces. I've got her buried down south of the pasture.

"I go out there sometimes." Boynton looked up, bleary eyed, at Cimarron. "You want to know what I do? I go out there and I curse over the spot where she's buried. I curse and I cry, drunk or sober, I do. I loved my Margaret more than any other woman in the whole wide world and I'll never forgive her for dying and leaving me. *Never!*"

Cimarron saw the tears well up in Boynton's eyes and spill over, to roll down his unshaved cheeks. He sat without moving as Boynton wept.

"Don't you ever love a woman like I loved my Margaret, son. If you lose her, it'll kill you sure as thunder follows lightning. But you'll do a lot of hurting first before you die."

Boynton raised the almost-empty bottle and waved it in the air. "This stuff's like laudanum. It takes the pain away, makes things all soft around the edges. Let's a man laugh a little at this old world and its wondrous ways." Boynton sobbed. He put the bottle down on the table. "But it wears off like it did a little bit ago when I fell out of bed and remembered that Margaret's dead and forgot how the hell I got home after being at Devine's Place last night—maybe somebody brought me in a wagon or maybe I walked all the way—and I don't know what day it is, and what's more, I don't give a good goddamn what day it is. How do you like those apples, son?"

"Boynton, you got chickens outside, but I didn't see any henhouse. Where do those hens go to set?"

"There's a kind of little cubbyhole under the north side of the house. They go in there. Why?"

Cimarron rose and went outside. When he returned, he was carrying four eggs. "You got a fry pan?" he asked Boynton.

"Try looking in that cupboard over there."

Cimarron did, and found the pan. After some more searching, he found a tin of lard near the sink. He took wood from the woodbox and began to build a fire in the cast-iron stove.

Boynton emptied his bottle and said, "Just what the hell do you think you're doing, son? You can't come into a man's home and act like it's all yours. Get the hell out of here!"

Cimarron melted some lard in the pan and then cracked the four eggs on its side and dropped them into it. While they sizzled, he found a clean plate in a cupboard and put it down in front of Boynton.

"Where are your eating irons?" he asked.

"In that there drawer."

Cimarron opened it and then placed a knife and fork beside the plate. When the eggs were ready, he slid them from the pan onto the plate and put the pan back on the cool part of the stove, regretting now that he had not been able to save some of the cow's milk.

"I'm not hungry," Boynton declared. He gave Cimarron a challenging glance.

Cimarron merely pointed to the plate.

Boynton picked up his knife and fork and began to eat. When he was finished, he said, "Why'd you go and do that?"

"Do what?"

"Fry me those eggs."

"Because you looked like you could use a square meal."

"Those eggs, they were real tasty." Boynton studied Cimarron's face a moment and then, "What's your name, son?"

"Cimarron."

"That's all?"

"That's all."

"Son, I'm sixty-six years old. I've lived long enough to learn that when a man takes a nickname for his moniker it usually means that name's a breastwork of sorts that he's set up for himself to hide behind for one reason or another. Is that the case with you?"

"Tell me about Archie Kane."

Boynton eyed the empty bottle, and then, anger distorting his features, he swung a hand and knocked it off the table.

The two men were silent as the bottle rolled along the wooden floor before coming to a stop against a wall.

Boynton said, "Kane comes to Catoosa now and then to rip and roar some. I've done my share of drinking with him. We met in Devine's Place one night some months back. He's not a real bad fellow when you come right down to it."

"But bad enough?"

"Kane let on to me that he's had a brush or two with the law in his time. But I didn't pry into what wasn't my business. That's not my way. He'd bought me more than my fair share of drinks, and that was good enough for me. Then he'd disappear for a spell before turning up again in Catoosa. Last time I saw him—it wasn't more than a few days ago, as I recollect—he seemed skittish as a colt in spring."

"Did he say what was making him nervous?"

"No. He just mentioned that he thought he'd best lie low for a spell."

"Where would he be likely to lie low?"

"You told me the truth before?"

"The truth about what?"

"About you wanting Archie to testify at a trial. I mean, you're not out to arrest him for anything he did, are you?"

Cimarron rummaged about in his pocket and found the summons. He handed it to Boynton, who read it and handed it back.

As Cimarron pocketed the summons, Boynton said, "He's got a place this side of the Verdigris River. It's about twenty miles south of Catoosa and nine, ten north of Broken Arrow. He lives there with his sister. If you were to ride southeast in a more or less straight line from here, you'd be sure to find it."

"Much obliged," Cimarron said, rising.

"Son, I want to apologize to you."

Cimarron stared at Boynton in surprise.

"For those terrible things I said about Margaret. I know in my mind she couldn't help it if she had tuberculosis and it took her. It's just that—well, in my heart I keep feeling like she went and betrayed me by dying. It's crazy."

"Not so crazy. A man's mind, it says one thing. At the same time, his heart, it shouts just the opposite."

"I still need her," Boynton whispered. "I still need her so bad like I did down all the years we were together."

Boynton dropped his head and then, raising it again, held out his hand to Cimarron.

Cimarron shook it and said, "Thanks for the information."

He left the house, stepped into the saddle, and headed southeast. As he rode, he spotted the wooden cross at the southern edge of the pasture that was made from two pieces of planking nailed together. As he passed it, he looked back over his shoulder and saw Boynton heading toward the grave that the cross marked, stopping now and then to pick buttercups.

Cimarron rode on. He looked back again and saw Boynton standing, a forlorn figure, beside his wife's grave, on which the buttercups he had picked lay like small fallen suns.

Boynton, Cimarron thought as he rode along, was trying to find a way to live with the pain that death had dealt him. Just as he himself was.

His hand rose and his fingers slid along the scar tissue that marred his face.

In his mind there arose unbidden an image of that long-ago day when he was but a small boy and he had lost his grip on the calf he had downed. He saw it running, bawling and searching for its mother, saw the cherry-red branding iron in his father's hand being swung recklessly and angrily, felt it scrape and sear and ultimately scar the side of his face. . . .

Cold sweat broke out on Cimarron's body as he rode on, remembering while trying hard once again to forget.

But the Texas bank he had been helping to rob on that day years later, after he had become a man, glowed ahead of him on the horizon.

He saw himself crouching to empty the huge iron safe; saw the sheriff come dashing through the door of the bank with a gun in his hand; saw himself instantly spin and fire; saw the sheriff, who, he realized only moments after firing, was the father he had not seen since running off from the homeplace many long years before that fateful meeting, fall; saw himself questioning the frightened patrons of the bank and learning that his father had drifted to the small Texas town after the death of Cimarron's mother and had taken the job of sheriff. . . .

Sweat soaked ino Cimarron's shirt, darkening it in places, as the images continued to careen through his mind.

He saw himself riding away from the bank—alone and stunned, saw himself drifting down through all the years afterward, trying to escape the memory of the dead face of his father gazing sightlessly up at him from the dusty floor of the bank. . . .

Always riding, always moving on, haunted by the ghost of the father he had unwittingly killed, which still stalked him across the plains and up into the mountains of his tormented mind.

An image flashed through his mind of himself being arrested in Indian Territory which had, in its odd and circuitous way, led to him being offered a chance to become a deputy United States marshal by Judge Isaac Parker and his realization that the stalking ghost of his father might finally be laid to rest if he were to take the job that Judge Parker had offered him, take the chance to secretly atone for his deadly deed, which he knew could never be undone but which he hoped might someday be redeemed.

He forcibly banished the images from his mind and thought again of Boynton and the man's battle with his own ghost. A losing battle? Maybe. No man won every battle he fought. Some ended in a draw. Some he lost.

Bitter knowledge, that. And he knew that he shared it with Boynton.

When he spotted the creek off to his left, he turned the dun and made for it. When he reached it, he dismounted and, after filling his canteen, drank some of the cool water as his horse walked out into it and bent its head to drink.

A crayfish scuttled backward on the creek bottom, stirring up mud into which it disappeared, and as it did, Cimarron noticed the overturned stones lying at odd angles on the creek's bed. Possum, he thought. Been feeding here. On crayfish.

He stood up and surveyed the surrounding area. Flatland mostly. There was a stand of blackjack oaks off to the west.

He looked down and began to examine the ground. He soon spotted tracks in a patch of bare ground bordering the creek. They confirmed his belief that a possum had visited the creek, probably during the previous night, since the tracks were fresh and the animal was a nocturnal type. The front feet had long thin toes splayed outward in a star-shaped pattern. The toes on the hind feet were even longer. They led down to the stream and then away from it, to vanish in the thick grass.

Cimarron studied the grass and finally spotted the possum's droppings. He glanced at the trees. That's where old possum will be taking his siesta, he thought. He led his horse toward the oaks and moved in among them, looking for the possum's daylight den. He found a few tracks and followed them to a deadfall that lay in a clump of brush, where they abruptly ended.

He kicked the deadfall twice in rapid succession.

The possum he had been tracking darted out of the end of the deadfall it had hollowed out, and raced to the nearest oak, which it quickly climbed.

Cimarron stared up at the possum's long, pointed snout, which was nervously twitching. The animal's hairless tail was wrapped tightly around a slender branch and its shaggy cream-white pelt made an easy target among the green leaves.

Cimarron unholstered his Colt, took aim, and fired.

The possum dropped, and he went over and picked it up by the tail.

He carried it back to where his dun was idly grazing, and hunkered down, pulling his bowie from his boot. After he had skinned and gutted the animal, he built a fire at a safe distance from the surrounding trees, using wood he had hacked from the deadfall that had been the possum's burrow. He spitted the carcass and held it over his almost-smokeless fire to roast, turning it slowly as its blood dripped down to sizzle in the low flames.

When the possum was cooked, he ate half of it and wrapped what remained in the empty grain sack he took from his saddlebag.

After kicking out his fire, he rode out of the thicket and continued traveling southeast. He had gone for no more than a mile when he spotted two riders topping a low ridge ahead of him and to the left. They were going at a gallop and they were too far away for him to make out their faces or even the clothing they wore.

In a helluva hurry, looks like, he mused as he watched them. The one up in front must have the horse with the best wind. The lead rider was some distance ahead of the one who was bringing up the rear.

Too bad they're not going my way, he thought. Might be nice to have a little company. As he rode on, the two riders disappeared behind the far side of the ridge.

Cimarron became acutely aware of the fact that he was again alone on the vast, apparently empty land. But it's the way, he thought, that I've spent most of my life so far. And it's more than likely the way I'll spend most—or maybe all—of what's left of it too. The prospect didn't please him.

When the log cabin came into view in the distance, he slowed his horse to a walk, and as he approached the building, he searched for signs of life near it and found none.

It was a small cabin. One-room affair, he guessed. No smoke rose from its turf chimney. There was a hitch rail out front to which a horse was tied. A pile of chopped wood was banked agaist one side wall and not far from the opposite wall was a three-sided log shed.

Boynton, Cimarron recalled, had said that Kane lived with his sister. Now that was interesting—or might turn out to be. Too bad, he thought, that I wasn't sent out here to bring Kane's sister back to Fort Smith to give some testimony at Munrow's trial. Too damn bad, but what the hell.

When he reached the cabin, he got out of the saddle, tied his horse to the hitch rail next to the horse already there, and went up to the door and knocked on it.

He waited and then knocked a second time.

"Kane!" he called out.

No one answered him.

He went back to the hitch rail, where the two horses stood with their heads hanging, braced his buttocks against it, and folded his arms over his chest. Wild-goose chase?

Maybe not. He had at least found where Kane lived. The man would have to come home sometime. But when?

The rifle shot almost got him.

Wood from the hitch rail spurted up into the air next to Cimarron.

He leaped toward his horse, pulled his Winchester from the saddle boot, and made a run for it. He had just turned the corner of the cabin when another shot slammed into the dirt behind him.

He hugged the cabin wall, reconnoitering. Where had the shots come from? The first one must have come from the west. If it had come from the east, his dun would probably be lying dead or wounded right now out in front of the cabin. The second one would have had to come from farther east to have gone past the end of the cabin's front wall.

He eased forward, keeping his back flat against the

rough logs behind him. From where he stood, he could see no one.

He removed his hat and dropped it on the ground before peering cautiously around the corner of the cabin.

That low rise out there. Little more than a big bump in the ground. But it was high enough to let a rifleman take cover behind it if he flattened himself down on the ground.

Had Kane come home?

Cimarron maintained his position, not moving a muscle, his eyes scanning the rise.

Movement—just above the soft grass topping it.

Somebody was running, crouching, just below the crest of the rise.

Planning on pinning me against this wall, Cimarron thought, like a deerskin pegged out to dry.

He was about to run for the rear of the cabin when the figure he had seen rose and a rifle rose up into the air.

Cimarron swung his Winchester up as a shot buried itself in the log wall behind him, and fired.

His attacker fell and rolled down the rise, coming to a stop at its base and lying there motionless.

Cimarron, after picking up his hat and putting it on, headed for the rise, his rifle at hip level, his finger on its trigger. He moved slowly, ready to fire a finishing shot if that became necessary.

A moment later, his eyes widened with the shock of what he saw. He swallowed hard.

He halted and stood staring down in dismay at the limp form of the woman he had shot.

Dead?

Cimarron stood stiffly as he stared down at the woman lying facedown in the grass, her left arm beneath her body, her right arm flung out as if she were reaching for something.

He'd never shot a woman before and he hated himself for having done so now.

Damnation!

But she had fired on him without cause, and what the hell was he supposed to do under the circumstances? Stand out in the open and let her gun him down like a chicken staked out to catch a cougar?

He hunkered down beside the woman. He put out his hand and then, uneasily, he withdrew it. But he had to know if he'd killed her.

He reached out again and his hand came to rest on her shoulder. She was warm. How long did it take a body to turn cold once it was dead? He turned her over as gently as he could. She flopped on her back like a dropped doll.

There was blood on her left side near her breast. It had made a sodden mess of the man's checkered shirt she was wearing. No wonder he'd thought he was trying to down a man. She was wearing jeans that were as worn as his own. Work boots. The Stetson she had been wearing lay a few feet away.

He placed the first two fingers of his right hand against her neck and sighed with relief because he felt a pulse beating there. He shifted her body slightly, trying to find out where he had hit her and whether the bullet was still in her body. His hand accidentally touched her breast as he stared down at the bloody wound in her side.

"Hey!" she said as she opened her eyes. "What're you trying to do to me?" She sat up and grimaced. "Take your hands off me, mister!"

"I wasn't—I was just—" What could he say to her? How could he explain. Should he tell her he was sorry? That would be worse than stupid—it would be silly. Could he say he hadn't meant to shoot her? No. Because he had meant to.

"I thought you were a man," he told her lamely, feeling oddly embarrassed. "I truly did."

"Do I look like a man to you?" She squinted at him. "Or are your eyes poorly?"

She didn't look like a man to him, not now, not up close. It was the clothes she was wearing. Put her in a halfway decent dress—blue, to match her eyes—and she'd be worth looking at, even if a man's eyes were poorly, as she had put it. Unbraid her brown pigtails, comb them out, wash her face some, touch up her regular features with a little powder and paint. . . .

"You didn't shoot me in the teat, so what were you doing with your paw on it?"

"I wasn't trying to take advantage of you, if that's what you're thinking. I was just trying to see—"

"I know what you were trying to see. If I hadn't of come to my senses when I did, you'd probably have had my pants down—and yours too. Don't think I passed out because you nicked me. What happened is, I lost my footing and fell and hit my head."

Cimarron had learned enough from his brief examination of her wound to realize that his bullet had gone through her flesh. "What you did," he told her, "is you fainted."

"You're an awful insultin' cuss, you are," she snapped. "I never fainted. Not once in my life did I ever. Not even the time I was snake-bit so bad and me no more than nine years old. I just whomped that old rattler's head off with my hoe and then set about knifing open my hand to suck the poison out so I could get on with my weeding."

Let it go, Cimarron advised himself. But she had very definitely fainted. He knew she hadn't simply fallen. And he knew her flesh wound wasn't bad enough to have made her lose consciousness.

"What were you doing prowling around my cabin?" she asked suspiciously.

"Wasn't prowling."

"You sure do look like a prowler with those glittery green eyes of yours and that scar on your face."

Cimarron sighed.

"Well?"

"Well, what?"

"You gonna confess to what you were doing when I threw down on you?"

"I was looking for a man—"

"What man?" she interrupted.

Cimarron sighed, more deeply this time. "I was looking for a man," he hurried on as she opened her mouth to speak again, "named Archie Kane."

"He's my brother. I'm Lila Kane."

"Pleased to make your acquaintance, Miss Kane."

"Forget the folderol. Call me Lila. It's a hateful name but I'm stuck with it. I truly wish my mama and daddy had named me something with a real ring to it. Something like Billie Jo or Bobbie."

"Can I help you down to the cabin?" Cimarron had been about to add her name to his question but decided against doing so, considering the sentiments she had just expressed concerning it.

"Haven't needed a man's help since the day I was born and don't expect to start needing it now neither." Lila got up. "Now, what the hell happened to my Sharps?" She went to her Stetson, picked it up, and rammed it down on her head.

"Up there," Cimarron said, pointing. "I'll get it for you."

She ignored his offer and strode up the hill to retrieve her rifle. When she returned, she walked past Cimarron as if he weren't there, heading toward the cabin, her rifle in the crook of her arm.

Cimarron watched her go, his eyes on her buttocks, which were neatly rounded beneath her tight jeans. Her figure, he noticed, was decidedly feminine beneath the masculine clothes covering it.

Not bad, he thought as he set out after her.

When he reached her side, she asked, "What're you looking for my brother for?"

"That can wait. We'd best, you and me, do what we can to fix you up where I ripped you open."

"I can take care of myself."

"I reckon you can . . . Lila. But I'd be glad to be of any help to you that I can."

"Then go fetch some water from the well back behind the cabin."

"Yes, ma'am."

"I told you once already. Cut out the folderol. Besides, I'm not married, so stop ma'aming me."

"Real glad to hear you're not, on account of that makes us two of a kind."

"I'm not one bit surprised to hear that you're not married. I mean, hell, who'd want to marry a scar-faced stag like you, is what I'd like to know."

Cimarron shrugged and, carrying his rifle, went around behind the house, where he lowered the oak bucket into the well. After hauling it up again, he carried the water he had drawn into the cabin.

He stopped abruptly as he came through the door, water sloshing out of the pail onto the dirt floor. "Well, I'll be damned."

"Like as not," Lila said matter-of-factly. "More'n just likely, I'd say, were I asked. A sure thing, probably."

She had her shirt off and her breasts—small, firm, and pert—were bare.

"Don't just stand there gawking at me. Set the bucket on the table. I've got to clean myself up."

Cimarron did as he was told and placed his Winchester on the table beside the bucket.

Lila dipped a none-too-clean cloth into the water and began to swab away the blood that was still oozing, but more slowly now, from her flesh wound.

"You're in the habit, I take it," Cimarron observed, "of going around in the nearly altogether in front of strange men."

"You're strange, all right. I noticed that fact the minute I first laid eyes on you while you were pussyfooting

64

around like a fox with his snout aimed at a coop full of hens."

Cimarron's eyes dropped from her breasts to the lithe body below them. It was firm and tautly muscled. She had a deeply set navel.

"In a minute you'll be starting to drool," Lila said sharply, and flung the bloody cloth into a corner. "Haven't you ever seen a woman's naked body before?"

"You're not entirely naked, and yes, I have."

"Never have been able to figure out why you men make such a fuss about catching a glimpse of these." She indicated her breasts as she reached up and took a small tin container down from a wooden shelf. "Or this." She patted her crotch.

"Well, a man has to start somewheres, and getting a glimpse is as good a place as any to start."

"Start what? Oh, I get it. Wrassling around until the fit passes."

"Wrassling?"

"Well, that's what men like to do with women, isn't it?" Lila began to apply salve to her torn flesh. "Or so I've heard tell."

"How old are you, Lila?" Cimarron figured twenty.

She replied, "Eighteen."

"You ought to put your shirt back on now."

"Why? It's hotter in here than in a cell in Yuma prison."

"Now, how would you know? About the cells in Yuma prison, I mean?"

"Heard talk. I listen close when people talk. That's how I learn things."

"You ever happen to hear people talk about how modesty becomes a woman?"

"Listen here, mister—you got a name, by the way?"

"Cimarron."

"Cimarron?" Lila repeated. "Well, Cimarron, you listen to me. I grew up with three brothers, each one rougher than the next. I learned to fight, ride, rope, shoot, and hunt, and I learned real good. Had to. It was root hog or die with those three rangy bastards I had me for brothers.

"Our parents, they were killed by Comanches when not

65

one of the four of us tads had yet hit ten. We made do. One way or another, we did. But the Comanches also got my youngest brother when he was twelve and out trapping. Whooping cough killed the middle one. Now there's just Archie and me left. He's seventeen.

"Wait! Don't say nothing. I'm not near finished yet. You wanted to know what I might've heard about a woman and her modesty. Well, I'll tell you something. When you're nine years old like I was when the Injuns killed our parents and you got three younger tads to see to, well, you stiffen your spine and you square your shoulders and you do what's got to be done to keep yourself and your brothers as hale and hearty as a blue-tick hound in his prime.

"I've wiped my brothers' snotty noses, cleaned up their messes when they got sick, broke open their boils, and horsewhipped their hides more times than I reckon you've sat a saddle. I've learned all there is to learn about men, and I can tell you I paid no more mind to those things dangling between my brothers' legs, were they limp or stiff, than a jaybird'd pay to a dead cat.

"So don't you go and talk to me about modesty. It's something I never could afford, not the way the four of us had to live. Modesty's something ladies who live in cities can afford."

Lila, her eyes blazing, pulled on her shirt and buttoned it.

"I wasn't finding fault with you," Cimarron told her. "I was just surprised to see you—well, the way you were."

"If you think I took off my shirt to rouse you, you're as wrong as a three-legged rooster. I took it off to make it easy to get at where I was hurt. If what I did's gone and given you any ideas, well, you can just get shut of them right now. I've never wrassled with any man before and I don't plan on starting to now, least of all with the likes of you."

"Well, we can be friends. I'm not a sore loser." Cimarron grinned and sat down at the table.

Lila stood glaring at him. And then, "That's a snappy rifle you've got." She sat down at the table and reached out to touch Cimarron's Winchester, which lay on the table between them. "I'd give my right arm and left leg for a gun like that."

"I'd consider giving you my rifle in trade—and for a lot less than your right arm and left leg." He grinned again.

Lila quickly withdrew her hand from the barrel of his Winchester. "You keep your gun and I'll keep my—modesty."

"But I hope you'll keep my offer in mind."

Lila, ignoring his remark, said, "That old single-shot Sharps of mine's not worth a tinker's damn compared to a repeater. It's ten years old now and I don't exactly fancy a fifty-four rim-fire. But I guess it'll have to do. Yours, it takes the same forty-four–forty cartridges as that Colt you're toting, don't it?"

"It does."

"That makes things a mite simpler. You don't have to carry around two kinds of ammunition."

"I like things simple. Makes life a little easier."

"Archie's not here."

"I can see that. Where is he?"

"Damned if I know. He rode out earlier today. Saw him and another man heading west when I was coming back from hunting. Didn't down a damned thing all day neither after walking my legs down to the nubs." Lila shook her head in disgust.

Cimarron remembered the two riders he had seen as he approached the cabin. "You don't know where your brother went?"

Lila shook her head. "He comes and he goes pretty much as he pleases. So do I."

Was that defiance he saw in her eyes? Cimarron wondered.

"You a friend of Archie's?"

"Nope. Got a summons for him. He's wanted back in Fort Smith.

"What for?"

If defiance had been in Lila's eyes earlier, Cimarron now saw it replaced by the wariness of an animal sensing a trap. "He's supposed to testify at Dade Munrow's trial."

"Him!"

"You know Dade Munrow?"

67

"Know enough about him to know I wouldn't get any closer to him than I would to a scared skunk."

"Bad man, is he?"

"No worse than any other, I guess. He's a horse thief, is what he is. Archie told me he saw Munrow a while back with a small herd of horses he'd stolen here and there. Munrow was selling them off to anybody'd buy them. He stole them up north near Dodge City and he was selling them down here."

"How did your brother know Munrow had stolen the horses?"

"Dade told him. They're friends, Archie and Dade are. Besides, anybody could've told those mounts was stolen. Archie said no two bore the same brand. Archie told me a deputy talked to him and he agreed to ride in and testify against Dade."

"You think maybe your brother changed his mind about testifying and ran off to keep somebody like me from collaring him and taking him back?"

Lila shook her head. "Archie probably didn't even know a lawman like you was out looking for him. You are the law, I take it."

"Deputy marshal."

"Where's your badge?"

"Don't wear one. Figured if I didn't, I'd be less conspicuous and less likely to scare away any game I happened to be stalking."

"That makes sense."

"Lila, where do you think Archie might've gone?"

"I've no idea, and that's a fact. Archie's wild. Restless, he is. Seventeen's a restless age for most men, I suppose. But lately he's seemed to me more than just plain restless."

"How so?"

"Skittish. Like the stock gets just before a bad storm hits."

"He tell you why he was feeling edgy?"

"No. But something was eating at him. I could tell. I know my brother. Maybe that's why he went and rode off with that man I saw him with."

"Who was the man?"

"I only saw him from a distance. Couldn't see his face."

Cimarron noticed the frown darkening Lila's face. "You're worried about Archie."

The frown was replaced by a scowl. "He's able to take care of himself. Ought to be anyway. Seventeen's a man's age. I can't keep looking out for him forever."

"When a woman loves a man—her brother, in this case—it must be hard for her to let him go his own way without doing her share of worrying about him. Especially if that woman happened to have raised that brother of hers all by herself."

Lila's features softened as she stared at the table, avoiding Cimarron's eyes. "Archie tends toward the wild side."

"And he isn't too choosy about who he takes as friends."

"I told you what I thought about Dade Munrow. There's others too who're just as bad. I warned Archie. But you know what he said to me when I told him to be careful? He said, 'Being careful's about as much fun as being a chicken out in the rain with the door to the coop closed.'"

"Maybe he'll settle down once he's done some more growing," Cimarron said.

"Maybe. Maybe not." Lila's frown returned, but then, as she looked up at Cimarron, she brightened and said, "You could talk to him when you find him. You could maybe tell him what happens to men who ride outside the law. You know."

"I know." Cimarron had almost whispered the words.

"So you could tell him—throw a real good scare into him."

"I don't tell other men how to live out their lives. Besides, you don't know a thing about me. I'm not the man to tell anybody what they should or shouldn't do, and you can believe me about that."

"But you're on the side of the law."

"I am now, yes."

"What's that supposed to mean?" Lila was studying Cimarron with clearly troubled eyes.

"Just what I said. No more. No less."

"You don't give a person an inch, do you?"

A bawdy thought scampered through Cimarron's mind. He quickly dismissed it. "I try hard to mind my own business. And my own business right now happens to be finding your brother and taking him back to Fort Smith. What's he look like?"

"He's tall. Tops six feet. Skinny as a snake. His hair's browner'n mine and his eyes are bluer. He keeps himself clean-shaven mostly."

"What was he wearing when he rode out?"

"Same as always. Jeans and boots. Blue shirt. Black vest."

"Well, I'd best be getting on his trail."

The scowl returned to Lila's face. "I don't relish asking anybody a favor, but if you find Archie—well, it wouldn't be all that much trouble, would it, for the two of you to stop by here before you head for Fort Smith?

"The least you could do is let me see Archie and find out if he's all right. I mean, that wouldn't put a burr in your britches, would it?"

"Nope. When I find him, I'll bring him back here before heading east."

"I don't expect something for nothing. I could give you something to take with you."

"Like what?"

"Food for the trail."

"Got me a big piece of roasted possum tucked away in my saddlebag. That ought to do me for a time before it goes gamy. Your brother's trail ought not to be too hard to find and follow."

Lila dropped her eyes.

Cimarron said, "Besides, you've already given me something to take with me."

She looked up at him, a quizzical expression on her face. "I have? What?"

"The memory of a real sweet-looking woman. Memories like that, they warm a man's heart."

Lila blushed, and then, obviously furious with herself for having done so, she snapped, "I don't want to be one of your memories."

"But you already are one. And I'll be able to separate you out from all the rest real easy."

Suspiciously, "How?"

"It'll be real easy, like I said. I'll remember you as the pretty one who wouldn't wrassle with me."

"You're damned right I wouldn't, and don't you forget it neither!"

"I'm not likely to." Cimarron touched the brim of his hat to her, picked up his rifle, and went outside.

He freed his horse, stepped into the saddle, and rode away from the cabin, heading north. He looked back over his shoulder as he topped the rise from which Lila had fired on him, but she was nowhere to be seen.

Well, he thought, a man can't be expected to score every single time. The trouble with you, though, old son, is you damn well do expect to score every single time and it gets to be tiresome when you don't.

When he reached the ridge on which he had seen the two riders whom he now believed to be Kane and the unknown other man that Lila had mentioned, he located their trail and followed it along the ridge until it dropped down the northern side.

They must be heading for Catoosa, he thought. Their trail leads in that direction.

He figured they were little more than an hour ahead of him. He could make up much of that. He slapped his dun's flank and the animal began to gallop. Funny thing about this trail, he thought as he rode, his eyes on the ground ahead of him. This is a real funny way for friends to ride. Single file. Like they weren't interested in talking to each other or maybe they were mad at each other.

It was dark when Catoosa's lighted buildings came into sight on the horizon, and Cimarron continued traveling at a gallop. As he rode into town, his eyes darted from one male face to the next, but none of the men he saw remotely resembled Kane as Lila had described him. Some were thin but bearded. Others were tall but heavy, even fat. A few were short.

He reined in his dun in front of Devine's Place and tethered it to the hitch rail beside several other horses. He eased his Colt out of its leather and then shoved it back down again. He repeated the move a second time, and then, when he was satisfied that his .45 would slide easily out of its holster, he entered Devine's Place.

The pool tables were surrounded by men. Two card games were in vigorous progress. The air was smoky, the sawdust even dirtier than it had been on his previous visit.

None of the men in the room was Kane.

Cimarron decided to make inquiries concerning Kane, but as he strode toward the nearest pool table, he remembered the back room. He glanced to the left. The door to the back room was closed. He went over to it and turned the doorknob. It wasn't locked. He opened the door and stepped into an even smokier room. Peering through the gray-blue clouds of smoke, he scanned the faces of the men standing at the makeshift bar.

Archie Kane stood near the far end of it.

Devine was behind it, and he frowned when he spotted Cimarron.

Cimarron gave him a friendly nod and then walked over to take a place at the bar next to Archie Kane. He was sure of his man, had been the instant he had first seen him a moment after entering the room.

Kane fit Lila's description of him perfectly. He was painfully thin, looking as if he hadn't eaten in a week. He looks, Cimarron thought, like he could take a bath in a rifle barrel. His dark-brown hair was shaggy, but he was clean-shaven. His eyes were a deep blue that bordered on black. He was wearing the clothes that Lila had mentioned.

"Howdy, Kane."

Kane started and glanced uneasily at Cimarron.

"You and me, we have some traveling to do together, Kane."

Kane stepped back from the bar, a fast move, and went for his six-gun.

But Cimarron's .45 had already cleared leather. It was in his hand and aimed directly at Kane.

"I didn't say we had some shooting to do, Kane. I said traveling. I'll relieve you of that gun."

"Who the hell are you?" Kane bellowed as he handed over his revolver. His boyish face was filled with fear as he looked from the gun in Cimarron's hand to Cimarron's face and then back down at the gun again.

He's ready to faint from fear, Cimarron thought as he shoved Kane's gun into his waistband. He's been expecting trouble. The minute I spoke to him he went for his gun without asking any questions. "Put your hands up high and then we'll mosey on out of here and I'll tell you who I am." No use, Cimarron thought, letting the other men in the room know who he was. News traveled fast. Too fast for comfort sometimes. The fewer people who knew that he was a lawman, the better he would like it and maybe the longer he would live.

"See here," Devine spluttered, pointing a finger at Cimarron. "I don't want any shooting in here. Get the hell out of here, both of you, and settle your quarrel outside."

"We're fixing to do that very thing," Cimarron said mildly without taking his eyes off Kane. "Kane, I promised your sister we'd pay her a visit before we move on."

"Lila? What's she got to do with this? Who are you, mister?"

Cimarron reached out, grabbed Kane's shoulder, and gave him a shove toward the door. As Kane went through it, Cimarron followed him into the larger room, where, when the men in it saw his drawn .45, they moved quickly out of the way.

Once outside Devine's Place, Cimarron said, "Now that was a ruckus that could've been avoided, Kane. I've got a summons for you."

"What's the charge?"

"No charge. You're wanted in Fort Smith. To testify against Dade Munrow at his trial. Now, I hope you don't plan on giving me any trouble on the way back because I surely will shoot you if you do and that won't make anybody happy. Not me. Not Judge Parker. Surely not you."

"I can't go to Fort Smith."

"Sure you can. Which one of these horses is yours?"

"I'm a dead man if I go back there to testify."

"You're a dead man if you don't."

"I got some money," Kane said. "Put that gun away and I'll give it to you."

"I know a youngster like yourself's got a lot left to learn, but you should have learned by now not to try to bribe a deputy marshal. Get on your horse, Kane."

"Twenty dollars," Kane said.

"Get on your horse. You don't, I'll wrap a rope around

you and you'll walk all the way to Fort Smith at the end of it."

"Can I put my hands down?"

"Put them down."

Kane did and went to the hitch rail.

Cimarron was aware of the men in the doorway behind him because he could hear their low voices. He thought of the rider who had been with Kane. He shifted position as Kane climbed aboard a bay gelding so that he wouldn't be liable to take a bullet in the back. Then, his Colt still in his hand, he reached out and untethered his dun.

As he holstered his Colt, Kane made a run for it, savagely spurring his gelding and racing down the street.

Cimarron sprang into the saddle and set out after him.

A cheer went up from one of the men standing in the doorway of Devine's Place.

Cimarron wasn't sure whether it was meant for him or for Kane.

He rode at a gallop, cursing Kane and cursing himself for having been careless enough to let the man get away from him.

Kane reached the end of the street and headed out onto the prairie.

Cimarron was closing the distance between them when he heard the shot. He didn't know where it had come from or who had fired it.

But then he saw Kane slump in his saddle and begin to slide from it. He looked behind him. There was no one in the street. The doorway of Devine's Place was empty. He looked up at the second floors of the few buildings that were taller than a single story on both sides of the street. He saw no one. The rooftops appeared to be empty.

He pulled his Winchester from the boot and kept it in his hand as he continued riding toward Kane, who had fallen from his horse, which had disappeared in the night.

Kane lay sprawled in the grass, and when Cimarron reached him, he quickly dismounted and put his horse between himself and the town. But he needn't have done so, he realized, because he was out of rifle range now of anyone shooting from the town.

Still, he didn't relax as he looked down at Kane. The man was alive.

But he wouldn't be for long, Cimarron was convinced.

He stared at the large and ugly hole that had been torn in Kane's chest only inches below his throat, where the bullet that had entered his back had exited.

Kane was pawing frantically at it, as if he were trying to close it with his bloody, grasping fingers.

He gasped, struggling for air to breathe.

Got him in the lung, Cimarron thought as he returned his Winchester to the boot.

He hunkered down beside Kane. "Who shot you? Do you know?"

Kane's lips parted and then closed in a grim line. They opened again almost at once and he wheezed, his chest heaving, his eyes on Cimarron's face.

"Can you talk, Kane?"

A slight movement of Kane's head from side to side was the only answer Cimarron got. Kane coughed up blood, which glistened wetly in the light of the moon.

"Was it the man I saw you riding with earlier today?" Cimarron asked.

Kane nodded and his eyes widened, but Cimarron could not read the message in them.

He swore. So this was to be the end of his first assignment. He'd finally found his witness only to have the man murdered right in front of his eyes. Some deputy marshal he was turning out to be, he thought bitterly and felt hatred for the unknown gunman welling up in him.

"Kane," he said, making one last try, "can you tell me the name of the man who shot you?"

Kane tried to speak, his eyes bulging with the effort. His lips quivered and blood trickled from between them.

Then the fingers of his right hand left his bloody chest and, trembling, rose in the air.

Cimarron stared at Kane's fingers, which were still fluttering above his chest. They continued to rise until they folded themselves together, all but the bloody index finger.

Cimarron looked in the direction Kane was pointing—at the sky.

And then he looked down again at Kane, whose pleading eyes were on his uncomprehending face.

Again Kane's lips opened but only a shallow wheeze slipped past them. His fingers continued to point upward. Cimarron looked up again and saw only the three-quarter moon and countless stars floating serenely in the night sky.

6

When Cimarron turned his head and looked back again at Kane, the man's hand fell to the ground. His eyes glazed and his chest no longer heaved.

Cimarron rose and stood for a moment staring down at the dead Kane, and then he looked up at the sky again.

What the hell had Kane been trying to tell him? He'd asked Kane if he knew who had shot him and Kane had responded by pointing to the sky.

Kane's gesture told Cimarron nothing. But he was keenly aware of the fact that Kane had been trying to identify his killer in the only way available to him, since he was unable to speak.

What now?

Well, one thing was sure: Kane wouldn't be testifying against Dade Munrow now. Cimarron decided that there was only one thing he could do. He'd take Kane back to Lila for burying.

But first . . .

He stared at the distant lights of Catoosa. The person who had killed Kane might still be there. And even more important, someone in Catoosa might be able to identify Kane's killer.

Maybe someone had seen what had happened, even though Cimarron himself had not seen anything.

A thought occurred to him.

Maybe the shot had been meant for him. He'd been ambushed once already since he set out from Fort Smith. Maybe the bushwhacker had followed him and tried a second time to kill him.

Maybe.

But he doubted it.

Kane had been a pretty fair distance ahead of him when the shot had been fired. The person who had fired it would have had to have been an awfully poor shot to have gone so wide of the mark, missing Cimarron and hitting Kane instead.

Still, it was a possibility that he had been the target and not Kane. It all depended upon the angle from which the shot had been fired.

Another thought occurred to Cimarron.

Maybe Kane's gesture had not been meant to identify the person who had shot him. Maybe it had been meant to identify the person who had fired at me, he speculated.

He remembered Adams. And Ella.

Maybe one of them had spotted him when he returned to Catoosa earlier, had waited for the right moment, and then gone gunning for him.

Maybe in the darkness they had mistaken Kane for him.

It seemed to Cimarron that a few questions were in order. He intended to ask them. There was no telling what he might find out.

He bent down, picked Kane up, and threw him over his saddle. Kane's hat fell off. Cimarron let it lie as he shoved Kane's body up tight against the saddle horn, boarded the dun, and headed back toward Catoosa. Kane wouldn't be needing his hat anymore.

He rode directly to Devine's Place and went inside, striding toward the door that led to the back room. He went through it and up to the bar.

"Devine," he said, "was Kane drinking alone in here a little while ago?"

"As far as I know, he was," Devine answered. "Now, see here. If you're intending to start more trouble—"

"I'm not. I'm fixing to find out the answers to a few questions I've got on my mind. Like, for example, did Kane have any enemies?"

"Most men have enemies."

"Answer the question, Devine, before I change my mind and decide to start more trouble, as you just put it—with you this time."

"I don't know!" Devine exclaimed, backing away from the bar toward the shelf that held his liquor bottles.

"Kane's dead!" someone shouted from the doorway. "He's draped over a horse outside like a sack of cornmeal and he's been shot dead!"

The room quieted. All eyes turned to Cimarron.

"I didn't shoot him," Cimarron said, breaking the sudden stillness. "But somebody sure did. What I'd like to know is *who* did. Or if the shot that killed Kane was meant for me. Now, then, what can you gentlemen tell me that I might find helpful?"

When no one spoke, Cimarron made a decision. He pulled the tin star from his pocket and held it up. "I'm a deputy marshal from Fort Smith. Now, I know you gentlemen find this here place a pleasure. But you and I both know it's an illegal operation that Devine's running here. Selling spirits in the territory's against federal law. I could close down this place—empty it out so fast you'd think it'd turned into a church on Saturday night. I could arrest Devine and charge you all with aiding and abetting his crime."

Cimarron suppressed the laughter that was gurgling within him as he thought of what he had just said. He had sounded to himself like a frontier lawyer as he talked about "aiding and abetting." A frontier lawyer with no more qualifications than the ability to read a little bit of Blackstone.

A man leaning against the far wall said, "Kane rode in here just before dark—alone."

"I'm not sure I follow you, friend," Cimarron said.

"Point is, he rode in here from the south only a few hours before he showed up a second time. The first time he came from the south, like I said. The second time from the north. There was another man riding with him the first time. I was just outside of town and I seen the other man holding a gun on Kane. He put it away when they got close to town.

"I followed them because I was curious. Well, once they got through town, which don't take long, seeing as how this's such a small place, the other fellow pulled his gun again and the two of them rode north."

79

"Kane in front?" Cimarron asked. "The other man riding a ways back?"

The man leaning against the wall nodded and suggested, "Maybe the one bringing up the rear was a lawman like yourself."

"Not likely. I was sent out to find Kane and take him back to Fort Smith. They wouldn't've sent another deputy out." Cimarron paused thoughtfully. "Did you get a look at the man riding behind Kane?"

The man Cimarron had addressed stepped away from the wall and, as he walked toward the bar, shook his head. "I didn't dare come too close to them. Figured it wouldn't be healthy for me if I did."

"Any of you gentlemen know why somebody'd be out gunning for Kane? Did somebody have a score to settle with him that you happen to know about?"

Silence.

Cimarron turned toward Devine. "Whiskey."

When a bottle and glass had been set in front of him, he filled the glass and emptied it in a single swallow. Maybe, he thought, it'll give me the courage I need when I next meet Lila and have to tell her about what happened to her brother.

He left Devine's Place after paying for his drink, and as he rode south through the darkness, he considered the information he had obtained. It was interesting but not conclusive of anything. It looked like somebody was out after Kane. Maybe Kane had given the man he'd been riding with the slip and the man had backtrailed, found him, and shot him to death.

Or had he himself been the gunman's target? Had Kane died by mistake? There was no way to fit the few facts he had together and come up with a sensible answer to explain what had happened, he concluded. Not if you considered the fact that he himself had been ambushed earlier by a would-be killer, there wasn't.

When he came within sight of the Kane cabin, he found it dark, as he had expected. He was not keen on waking Lila to present her with the grim news of her brother's murder.

It could wait until morning.

Cimarron got out of the saddle, placed Kane's body on

the ground, stripped the gear from his horse, and hobbled it. Then he made his own bed and climbed into it.

A harsh metallic sound woke him the next morning. He immediately reached for his Colt, which lay on the ground beside him. He looked around and saw that he was alone. He raised himself up on his elbows and gazed at the cabin.

The sounds he was hearing were coming from the cabin's vicinity and he knew now what they were. Someone was working in the three-sided shed—hammering iron.

He shook out his boots and pulled them on. Then his hat. He got up and took the portion of roasted possum from his saddlebag and began to eat it as he listened to the harsh sound of hammering that was shattering the midmorning air.

When he finished eating, he put his gear back on his horse, threw Kane's body over the saddle, and then, leading the dun, walked toward the shed, his expression grim.

He left the dun beside the shed and walked around it.

Lila, wearing a leather apron, was bent over behind a horse. She had its left rear foot locked between her knees and she was hammering a shoe into place.

Cimarron hesitated. He couldn't greet her with a "good morning." It wasn't—or wouldn't be—a good morning for her when he told her his news. He settled for "Lila."

She looked up at him from where she stood beside the blazing forge and quickly pulled the nails that she was holding in her teeth from her mouth. "You're back."

"I am."

"You found Archie?"

"Yes."

"Easy, boy," Lila said as the horse nickered and shifted its weight. She resumed her work, remarking, "You should have seen the sorry condition this beast was in when the man who owns him brought him in yesterday. The walls of his hooves were all outgrown and in need of a whole lot of paring. Nails were practically hanging out of the shoes he was wearing so that it's a wonder he could even stand, let alone walk."

81

"Where'd you learn to be a farrier?" Cimarron knew he was stalling.

"Oh, hell, somewhere along the line." Lila put the horse's foot down and moved to the opposite side of the animal. She lifted the unshod right foot and placed it between her knees. She picked up a cooled shoe from the anvil and placed it against the horse's foot.

"The last person who worked on this beast shoed him all wrong. See here how square his toes are?" Without waiting for a response from Cimarron, she continued, "He was wearing *rounded* shoes!" She shook her head in disgust.

"Dammit!" she muttered as the nail she was hammering bent and fell to the ground. "He's got a broken wall on this hoof, which makes it harder'n finding a sliver of ice in the whole of hell to get him shod right. I had to heat these shoes and hammer the hell out of them to get them to fit snug."

Cimarron watched her admiringly as she deftly continued nailing the right shoe into place.

"There," she said, lowering the horse's foot to the ground. "Sweaty work," she commented, wiping her dirty forehead with the back of her equally dirty hand. "Where's Archie? In the cabin?"

Cimarron shook his head. "Outside."

"Well, why doesn't he come on in and join the party? Hey, you old Archie Kane, you!"

"Lila—"

She placed the hammer on the anvil and stared at Cimarron, her eyes narrowing. "What's wrong?"

"Lila, I ran into Archie in Catoosa. He was edgy, like you said. He made a run for it. I went after him." Cimarron fell silent, looking at the ground.

"What happened?" Lila's words had been sharp stones she had thrown at Cimarron.

"He's dead. Somebody shot him."

"Somebody . . . *you!*" she screamed.

As she came at him, Cimarron raised his hands to ward her off, but she was on him, pounding his chest with her fists and then trying to land a fist on his jaw.

"You lied to me!" she screamed. "You didn't want him

to testify at any trial. You knew he had helped Dade steal those horses! You—"

Cimarron seized her wrists.

She drew back her right leg and booted him in the knee. He gritted his teeth as he turned her and pinioned both of her arms behind her back. Her pigtails whipped his face as her head bobbed violently back and forth during her struggle to free herself.

"I didn't kill him, Lila. I told you the truth."

"Liar!"

"I'm not lying to you. You can go to Catoosa. You can ask around. Somebody, no doubt, saw what happened. They can tell you that I didn't kill Archie."

Lila went limp.

If Cimarron hadn't been holding her so tightly, she would have fallen.

"Lila? You all right?"

She drew a deep breath, and as she straightened up, Cimarron released her.

She took a step forward and then her shoulders slumped.

She placed both hands on the anvil and leaned heavily upon it.

Cimarron waited for her tears.

They never came.

"He was the last," she murmured. "He was all I had left of my family. Now there's only me."

Cimarron could think of nothing to say, nothing that would help to soothe her, certainly nothing that could change the ugly way things were for her now.

She turned to face him. "Where is he?"

"Behind the shed. On my horse."

Lila swiftly left the shed.

When Cimarron caught up with her, she was standing behind the shed, staring in silence at the corpse of her brother.

"I'll kill whoever did this to him," she said huskily. "With my two bare hands, I'll kill him. He wasn't but a boy. He was just seventeen. He had so much living left to do."

Cimarron, standing beside her, said, "He tried to tell

me who shot him. At least, I think that's what he was trying to tell me."

"What did he say?" Lila's hand reached out and came to rest on her brother's shoulder. She stroked it gently.

"He couldn't talk," Cimarron said. "But when I asked him if he knew the man who'd shot him, he pointed at the sky."

Lila suddenly threw herself against her brother's body, gripping it tightly in both arms, her left cheek pressed against his back just below the point where the bullet had entered it.

Cimarron listened to her sobs and watched helplessly as her body convulsed and she fought back the tears that finally came, a salty flood that made gray streaks on her dirty cheeks.

She released her hold on her brother and stepped back, tossing her head in a way that made Cimarron think of an unbroken mustang.

"I'm acting like a damn-fool woman!" she declared angrily.

"You're acting like anybody else'd act whose been bad hurt, woman or man, if him or her had an ounce of decent feeling in them."

"I got me some burying to do," Lila said. "I'll go get a shovel.

Lila stood silently beside the covered-up grave Cimarron had helped her dig. The sun was setting and her shadow fell across the grave as if to embrace it.

"I could have dug it by myself," she muttered.

"You could have, I've no doubt, but I figured the least I could do was to lend you a hand in this sorry matter."

"There's no reason for you to hang around here now. Archie's dead. You can't take him anywhere now. So why don't you light a shuck and get on out of here and leave me be?"

"I wanted to have a talk with you. But maybe now's not the time. How about tomorrow?"

Lila thrust her hands into the pockets of her jeans. "I got nothing I want to say to you, nothing at all. So you can just fork your horse and get going. I've got work to do." She strode away from the mounded earth and headed back toward the cabin.

Minutes later, Cimarron saw her round the shed leading the horse she had shod. She made for the hitch rail in front of the cabin; she untethered the horse that was tied to it and rode away to the west, leading the recently shod horse.

She didn't return until well after midnight and she said nothing to Cimarron who was sitting on the ground with his back braced against the cabin wall as she tied her horse to the hitch rail.

She walked past him and went into the cabin.

When light streamed from its windows, Cimarron got up and entered the cabin.

Lila had lit a coal oil lamp and she was sitting at the table with her hands folded upon it. She didn't look up as he came into the room.

He stood just inside the door, his thumbs hooked in his cartridge belt.

She was, he noticed, wan and her face was drawn. Resignation was clearly etched on her features. She seemed to have aged. He glanced at her strong capable hands. They were nicked and scratched and almost as callused as his own.

"You ought to get some sleep," he told her. "I'll bed down outside."

"No need to do that," she surprised him by saying. "There's two beds in here, as you can surely see. That one's mine over there near the door and that one up against the wall is—was—Archie's. You can use it, if you don't mind sleeping in a dead man's bed."

"I've slept in worse places in my time with my back for a mattress and my belly for a blanket." Cimarron hesitated a moment and then drew Kane's six-gun from his waistband and placed it on the table.

"Archie's," Lila said, staring at it.

Cimarron went over to the bed set flush against the wall and unstrapped his cartridge belt, which he eased under the bed. Then he sat down on the bed and pulled off his boots. He lay back on the bed, locking his hands behind his head, staring up at the shadows skittering across the ceiling which were created by the flickering flame of the lamp.

Minutes passed.

"I shouldn't have raised such hellfire with you, when you came back here," Lila said at last, her voice little more than a whisper.

Cimarron turned his head, but because her back was to him, he couldn't see her face. Her head was bowed.

"What happened before—it was my fault," she said. "From the minute you told me you were hunting Archie I suspected that you weren't laying it all on the line with me. I figured for sure you were after him for horse stealing. So when you came back and told me he'd been killed, I was sure you'd done it."

"And now you're not sure, is that it?"

"I did like you said I should do. After I delivered that horse I shod to the man who owns it, I rode into Catoosa. I met a man there by the name of Boynton. He told me he heard what happened because everybody was talking about it. Nobody saw the man who shot Archie, he said. But the point was, nobody, he said, saw you shoot him. Boynton, he had kind words to say abut you."

"I'm glad you found out what you did from Boynton. I didn't at all like you thinking of me as a murderer."

"You needn't act so pious with me," Lila said, her temper flaring. She turned around in her chair to confront Cimarron. "From the minute I first laid eyes on you I had you figured for a killer. There's something about your eyes, and I don't mean their color. I mean the hard way you have of looking at a person. Like you can see right through them and you don't like what you see."

"I've killed men, that's true."

"Knew it."

"But I never drew first. The only times I've killed was because I had to, else I'd of been dead myself. Mind now, I'm not bragging. Just telling the truth. I'm not the least bit proud of having had to kill men more than once."

"I lied to you, you know."

"I know you did. You lied by not telling me the whole truth about your brother. When I brought him back here, you said he'd been in on the horse-thieving with Munrow."

Lila dropped her eyes. "He was in on it. But when a deputy finally caught up with Munrow, he told the deputy about Archie's part in the deal. Then Archie told the deputy that Dade was a liar and he said he'd be glad to testify against Dade. Archie told the deputy he'd seen Dade steal the horses. The deputy believed Archie and he said they'd send somebody for him when the trial was to be held. A deputy did come here later with a summons for Archie, but Archie never did go to Fort Smith."

"How long had Archie been riding the owl-hoot trail?"

"Since he was fourteen. We were living up north of Dodge then. That's where he first met Dade. I tried my damnedest to straighten him out, I can tell you. I truly did. I thrashed him within an inch of his life once when he was fifteen. It didn't do no good. None at all. Then, before long, Archie and Dade, they had the law after them. They ran. I ran with them."

Lila looked up at Cimarron, who was watching her closely. "Well, Archie was all I had left. I'd already buried two brothers, like I told you. I felt like I had to go with him. The trouble was, you see, I had hope. I hoped I'd find one way or another of straightening out that bastard of a brother of mine! But I never did!"

Cimarron was silent as Lila broke down and wept.

When she had recovered a few minutes later, she said, "Dade it was who wanted to come down here into the Nations, where there was a lot less law than there was up around Dodge. Besides, he'd started telling Archie about Jim Reed's gang and about all the hell they were raising down here. Archie was eager as a crow eating corn to join the Reed gang. He did. Him and Dade."

It was all beginning to make sense to Cimarron. "Looks to me like somebody came here to get Archie to keep him from testifying against Munrow."

"They intended to kill him?" Lila shook her head in denial. "That don't make any kind of sense. Whoever came for him could have gunned him down right here at the cabin."

"Maybe they just wanted to keep him under wraps for a while. Without his testimony, I was told, the prosecuting attorney back in Fort Smith didn't have a hope in hell of convicting Munrow."

"Archie must've gotten scared of whoever took him away from here," Lila speculated. "Maybe he thought the man was going to kill him. So he found a way to escape from him. Only it didn't work. The man must've back-trailed him and shot him to death once he saw that you'd gotten your hands on Archie."

"That's the way it looks to me from where I sit—lie." Cimarron tried a smile, but Lila's set features didn't soften. "What do you know about this Reed gang? Who's Jim Reed?"

"Reed's dead. But some folks still call the border scum who used to ride for him the Reed gang. They're still riding, like I said. Only now the gang's run by a woman. Her name was Myra Belle Shirley until she married Reed. He got himself shot to death by Sheriff John T. Morris. That was back in seventy-four."

"Never did hear tell of this Reed woman."

"Archie and Dade, they used to joke that her name wouldn't stay Reed for long. It seems that Myra Belle's got her cap set for one of the men who rides for her—a Cherokee bandit name of Sam Starr. You ever hear of him?"

"Can't say as I have."

"Mean man, Starr," Archie used to say. He claimed Starr was mean enough to share his dinner plate with a rattler."

Starr!

"Lila!" Cimarron suddenly exclaimed, sitting up and swinging his legs over the side of the bed. "That might be it!"

"Might be what? What the hell do you happen to be talking about?"

"Listen to me now and listen good. I told you that Archie, just before he died—I asked him who shot him, asked him did he know who'd done it. I told you he pointed to the sky. It was night at the time. I couldn't figure out for the life of me what he was trying to tell me. But maybe he wasn't pointing at the sky. Or at the moon that was in it. Maybe he was pointing at the stars! *A* star! Maybe he was trying to tell me that Sam Starr you just mentioned done him in!"

Lila's face had become animated as she listened to Cimarron. "I'll bet my bottom dollar that's what Archie meant! It's just got to be, don't you see, Cimarron? I mean, what he did, it couldn't mean anything else, now could it?"

Cimarron didn't reply immediately as he fancied he heard the echo of his name, which Lila had just addressed him by for the first time since they had met.

"I'll bet you're right! Archie was riding with the Reed gang, him and Dade was. He knew Starr. And Starr knew him. It all fits, Cimarron!"

The second time.

Cimarron said, "I think I ought to go look up this Sam Starr. Have a talk with the man. Did Archie tell you where the Reed gang goes to ground?"

"They're headquartered, he said, in Claremore."

"Claremore," Cimarron repeated. "That's northeast of Catoosa, as I recall."

"It is."

"Well, I'll be heading for Claremore, then."

"You don't mean right now, do you?"

"Nope. But as soon as day breaks I'll set out."

Lila blew out the lamp and Cimarron heard her moving through the darkness that filled the room. He heard her throw herself down on her bed. He lay back on his own bed and turned toward the wall.

He closed his eyes.

But he couldn't sleep. Thoughts of the Reed gang raced through his mind. Thoughts of Lila lying not far from him overflowed it.

He felt a tightening sensation in his groin. But he made no move. She'd just buried her brother. She was grieving. Maybe some other time. But not now. Besides, she was a tough one. Mean enough to hunt bear with a switch. Were he to try to take her on, he might find himself—damn well would find himself, he believed—astride nothing but trouble.

But she was, after all, a woman, wasn't she? Underneath those he-man duds of hers, was—

He sighed audibly.

"What's the matter?" asked Lila from her bed near the door. "Can't you sleep?"

"Nope." Never mind why.

"I've been thinking."

"What about?"

"You."

Her answer surprised him. "Nice thoughts, I hope."

"I've been thinking I owe you and I don't like being beholden to anybody, least of all to a man."

"Now, why would you go and think a thing like that?"

"You brought Archie back to me. You didn't have to. Many's the man who'd've left him lying right where he fell. But I've no way to pay you back for what you did."

"No need to pay me. I did what seemed decent, is all."

"What I've been thinking about, though, it's an *indecent* thing to do. Everybody says so."

Cimarron flopped over on his back. "Honey, I don't seem to be able to follow you."

"Don't you 'honey' me. You're laying over there thinking the same damned thing as I am. Don't try to deny it."

"I admit I've been thinking you're a fine figure of a woman."

Lila harrumphed. "But anyway, like I said, I'm in a spot, owing you like I do."

"Lila, you don't owe me a thing. Now forget it and let's both of us try to get some sleep."

Cimarron turned toward the wall again.

"You want to wrassle?"

Lila's question caused Cimarron to sit up, already stiffening. "You coming over here or do you want me over there?"

"You stay put. You'd most likely break your leg trying to navigate across this dark room. I'm coming over there."

Moments later, she was standing beside Cimarron's bed. She gave him a shove toward the wall. "This bed's narrow as a buggy whip." She lay down on her back beside him. "I'm ready," she said, and this time it was she who sighed.

"No, you're not," Cimarron whispered. "Listen, honey, this's no good. You got to want to—wrassle. It's not a way of balancing the books between a man and a woman. Now, don't get me wrong. I appreciate your offer, I truly do and I'd like to accept it. But you're going about this the wrong way, believe me."

Lila began to cry.

Cimarron frowned in the darkness, feeling the warmth of her fully clothed body next to his own. "I didn't mean to offend you, honey."

Sobbing, Lila said, "It's not only that I owe you. It's not just that. It's that I loved Archie best of all my brothers and now he's gone and I feel like part of me's buried out there with him.

"Laying over there, I felt so all alone. I felt like I needed something living to snuggle up to so's I wouldn't feel so—so fearful of things."

Cimarron reached out and found her face. He leaned over and kissed her wet cheek. "Dealing with the dying of somebody you love's a hard business."

"I shouldn't be acting like this on account of I've had practice dealing with loved ones dying on me. Too much practice, and that's the sad fact of the matter!"

"Honey, are you sure—"

"I didn't come over here for you to try to talk me to sleep. I came for comforting, dammit!"

Cimarron began to unbutton her shirt, planning to comfort her the best way he could. He unfastened the buttons of her jeans and then said, "Lift yourself up some so's I can slip them off."

"Wait! I got to get my boots off first."

Cimarron propped himself up on one elbow as Lila sat up. Then he got up and slipped out of his clothes and got back on the bed. When Lila lay down beside him, his tentatively caressing fingers confirmed the fact that she was as naked as he was.

Lila suddenly seized him in an iron grip, using both of her arms.

"Hey!" he exclaimed, startled.

"Is this how I go about it?" she asked him, squeezing harder.

"Not exactly," he said somewhat breathlessly.

"How *do* I go about it?"

He told her and was about to ease himself into her when he remembered what she had told him: *"I've never wrassled with any man before and I don't plan on starting to now, least of all with the likes of you."*

91

"Honey," he said softly, "I hate to tell you this but you're going to hurt some at first."

"I am? Then, why do people do it if it hurts them?"

"It doesn't hurt men. Just women and just the first time, as a general rule. If you're scared, you just say so and we'll call it quits real quick. I don't want to hurt you."

"You think I'm scared, do you? Well, I've been burned by fire, bit by a snake, banged into by a buggy, and shot by you. I'm not scared. *Where* will it hurt?"

Cimarron, suppressing his amazement, answered, "Right down here where I am at the moment."

"I've never been hurt *there* before," Lila said, a sense of wonder in her tone.

"You'll bleed a bit."

"The ticking on this old straw pallet's been wanting a washing for nigh onto a week now. What are you waiting for?"

She was as dry as good tinder, but Cimarron decided to go ahead anyway. He braced himself and then plunged into her, intending to get it over with as quickly as possible.

Lila made no sound.

"Honey, you all right?"

"I'm fit as a fiddle. I don't call that kind of little twinge *hurting*. I call that—"

Cimarron kissed her lips, silencing her as he gently probed her. Arching his back, he partially withdrew from her, then slowly reentered her, and withdrew again.

Lila pulled her head away from him and said, "You're sunfishing like a green mount."

"Reckon I am. But that's the way a man has to go about this business. One way to go about it, at any rate."

"How many ways are there, all told?"

Before Cimarron could respond, Lila groaned and a moment later she moaned, a long, drawn-out sound.

Cimarron kept at it as her legs encircled his thighs. "You're catching on quick," he whispered to her.

"I feel awful funny," she said. "Way down deep inside." She moaned again and wrapped her arms around Cimarron's body, holding him tightly against her. "I feel like I'm going to—"

"I hope you are, honey."

She cried out then, her body shuddering beneath Cimarron, her hands gripping his shoulders.

Cimarron, who had been holding himself back, now let himself go, sweating, eagerly kissing Lila's cheeks and lips, nibbling at her earlobes.

"Oohhhh!" she cried as he exploded within her. "Oh, my!"

Cimarron's body gradually shuddered into stillness. He lay upon Lila for a moment, breathing heavily, and then he raised his head and shook his hair out of his eyes.

"What comes next?" Lila asked him eagerly.

He spent most of what remained of the night answering her question.

7

"We had us more fun last night than two pups in a basket," Lila declared happily late the next morning as she stood in front of the stove frying sowbelly and boiling beans.

Cimarron grinned and said, "We did, now, didn't we?"

"That was like no wrassling match I've ever been in in my whole life," she exclaimed as she flipped pieces of sowbelly in the pan.

"It's more a second cousin to wrassling, is what it is," Cimarron told her.

"But it was more than just a whole lot of fun for me," Lila said, suddenly serious. Avoiding Cimarron's gaze, she added, "It was comforting, you and me being together like that, just like I hoped it would be. But not exactly in the way I expected it to be."

Cimarron took the steaming coffeepot from the stove and filled a cup. He sipped from it and then said, "It's a real fine way for a man and woman to get close to each other—in more ways than one."

"I still feel kind of close to you now on account of what happened last night. It's a feeling I've never once felt before. It's nice."

"I know what you mean. A friendly feeling."

"Something a little bit more than just friendly," Lila said shyly. She forked a large piece of sowbelly onto a plate and handed the plate to Cimarron. As he sat down at the table, she said, "I haven't had much time for feelings in my life, friendly or otherwise. I always seemed to have too much to do. Lately, with working as a farrier to try to make ends meet and worrying all the time about Archie . . ." She fell silent.

Cimarron looked down at the sowbelly on his plate. Burned. As Lila spooned beans onto his plate, he refused to let himself grimace. They were shriveled up as a result of having been overcooked.

"Eat up," she ordered.

He tried to.

"You're not hungry?" she asked, standing over him. "I'm starved."

Cimarron managed to down a few beans and a relatively uncharred piece of sowbelly.

Lila filled a plate for herself and then sat down next to him. She ate heartily and in silence for several minutes before remarking, "It's a fairly long ride up to Claremore." She jabbed her fork at Cimarron and said resolutely, "I'll ride along with you to keep you company."

He looked up at her in surprise. Then, uneasy, he searched for a way to dissuade her from pursuing her plan. "People see you with a scar-faced man like me, they'll figure you just couldn't do any better for yourself."

"I'm real sorry I called you scar-faced the day we first met."

"Well, it's true, I am scarred." In more ways than one, Cimarron thought. He managed to swallow another small piece of sowbelly.

"Can you write?" Lila asked him, and when he nodded, she said, "I'll bet you can even read, can't you?" When he nodded a second time, she said, "You'll write a note for me. Write down that I had to go away for a spell. I'll nail it on the door so that if anybody comes by here with a horse needing shoes they'll know I'm not to home."

"Lila, you can't come with me."

"Why the hell not?"

"Well, for one thing, it's going to be dangerous, what I'm fixing to mix myself up in."

"I can hold up my end of things. All I need is my Sharps and Archie's sidearm."

Cimarron pushed his chair away from the table and watched her as she emptied her plate. This trail he was on had suddenly taken an unexpected twist, to put it mildly.

"The two of us," Lila declared, "we'll gun down the

whole Reed gang. What a team we'll make, you and me, Cimarron. We'll be hell on the border and then some!"

"I'm going after the man who killed your brother," Cimarron told her. "There's likely to be trouble. Shooting. Killing."

"Good! I hope I'm the one who gets to drop the bastard who killed Archie. You can take all the rest of them."

"Lila, I can't let you come with me. You stay put right here till I come back. I will come back. I promise you that."

"Cimarron—"

He shook his head. "I don't want to take a chance on you getting yourself hurt. I want to be sure you'll be here when I get back."

She pursed her lips and glared at him. "You don't want to have anything to do with me no more."

"Honey, it's not that." He reached out and patted her hand.

Angrily, she slapped his hand away.

"'Heaven has no rage,' " he quoted, " 'like love to hatred turned, nor hell a fury like a woman scorned.' "

"What're you auguring about now?"

"Those are some words from a play I read once and learned by heart. A man named Congreve wrote them."

"You sounded to me like you were talking in a foreign language or something. I didn't understand a single word you said."

A good thing she hadn't, Cimarron thought. If she had understood, she would probably have been provoked even more than she was already, and the last thing he needed right now was a provoked woman getting peevish with him.

"If I rode along with you," she said, "it'd be a lot better than you going up against the Reed gang all alone. Two's better odds than just one."

"No!" Cimarron said firmly. "You're going to stay here and shoe your horses and do whatever else there is to be done around here until I get back."

"What makes you think you can catch the man who killed Archie all by yourself?"

"I'll catch him."

"Maybe you will. Only I could help—"

"No, honey!"

Lila looked down at her empty plate for a moment and then up at Cimarron. Her hand came out from under the table and she placed it on top of Cimarron's which was resting beside his plate. "You're not such a bad-looking fella even with that scarred face of yours. But you wouldn't be so good-looking were you to go and get yourself killed."

"I plan on staying alive awhile longer."

"I got to confess it. I sure as hell hope you do."

"So us two pups can climb back in that basket you spoke about a little bit ago?"

She gave him a radiant smile.

And then she followed him outside and watched as he got his dun ready to ride. She stood with folded arms, leaning against the cabin wall, her eyes wistful, her expression morose.

"Cimarron, are you bound and determined not to change your mind about letting me ride with you?"

"I'm bound and determined."

She muttered an oath, bringing a grin to Cimarron's face. He went over to her and placed his hands on her shoulders. For a moment, she looked as if she were about to shake them off. But she didn't. She simply stood there, looking up into his eyes.

He said, "Now you take real good care of yourself, honey. I want to see you as frisky as a colt on a frosty morning when I get back here."

"I don't mind if you feel you got to kiss me good-bye."

He bent down and kissed her.

When their lips parted, Lila said, "That tongue of yours is almost as long as your—as a garter snake."

He kissed her again and then stepped into the saddle and turned his dun away from the cabin. He rode north, turning twice to wave to Lila, who returned his wave each time, her hand vigorously cleaving the air above her head.

Then he rode down the rise, and the cabin and Lila were lost to sight.

He neared Claremore at sundown, and as he rode into the town, he saw four men come stumbling out of the rear

97

of a building that had a sign in front of it reading: DRY GOODS. He watched the men climb clumsily into the saddles of their horses, which were grazing behind the building, and start riding toward him, their guns drawn and firing repeatedly into the air.

As the obviously drunken men went yip-yipping at the top of their lungs past him, Cimarron got down from his horse and tethered it in front of the dry-goods store. He went inside and spoke to the clerk behind the counter.

"Where might a man buy himself a drink in this town?" He was fairly certain that he knew the answer to his question. The four riders he had just seen had answered it for him.

The clerk eyed him somewhat suspiciously and then jerked a thumb over his shoulder. As Cimarron headed for the rear of the store, the clerk said, "That door's kept locked. You have to go outside and around to the back door."

Cimarron did and soon found himself in a crowded room. As he shouldered his way through the crowd toward the bar at the rear of the room, a woman wearing a low-cut red velvet dress hooked her arm in his and said, "Hello there, cowboy. I'll bet you'll buy me something to quench this terrible thirst I seem to have developed."

"I will," he said amiably. "What'll it be?"

When they reached the bar, she said to the bartender, "Mike, I'll have beer if it's cold. Whiskey if it isn't."

When Cimarron ordered whiskey, the woman turned toward him with a tired smile. She was buxom—large breasts, broad hips, solid arms and thighs. Surprisingly dainty feet in satin slippers. She was pale, partly because, Cimarron noticed, she had chalked her nose and cheeks. Her eyes were a bit too bright. She had a thin nose that looked like it could slice cheese. Full, moist lips.

"You're a big man," she commented, her smile threatening to sag at any moment.

"All over."

Her smile recovered as she widened her eyes in mock shock. "I don't know whether to believe you or not."

"Don't matter if you do or don't. But it's the truth I told you."

She picked up a glass of beer the bartender placed in

front of her and raised it to her lips. Gazing at Cimarron over the rim of her glass, she said, "I could call you. Ask for proof of your claim."

Not now, Cimarron warned himself. Lila's just about worn me out. "I'm looking for somebody."

"So am I. I think I might have found him."

"I'm looking for a woman."

She put her beer down on the bar and pretended to pout.

"Her name," Cimarron said, "is Myra Belle Shirley—I mean, Myra Belle Reed."

"My name's Tess."

"You know her?"

"What's your name?"

Cimarron downed his whiskey and then turned away from Tess to scan the faces of the men in the room.

"No need to shy away from me like that," Tess said, her hand coming to rest on Cimarron's forearm. "Names don't matter very much here in the territory. Anyway, it wasn't your name—whatever it might be—that attracted me to you in the first place. Do you want to know what did attract me to you?"

Cimarron continued to scan the room in silence.

"It was the way you walked."

"The way I walked?"

"Like this." Tess squared her shoulders and, letting her arms dangle at her sides, took a few steps, her body loose and swinging lithely.

She returned to Cimarron and said, "I saw a mountain lion walk that way once. He was also all muscle and strong bone."

"You'll have to excuse me, Tess. I got to find out if anybody around here knows where I can find Mrs. Reed."

Before he could move away from her, Tess said, "I know where you can find her."

"Where?"

"Not in Claremore. Not anymore."

"Then where exactly?"

Tess smiled and cocked her head to one side. "I can't tell you where *exactly*. But I can give you a general idea of where she is. She left Claremore almost a week ago, her and her boys. They were heading, I'm told, for Tulsey Town."

Cimarron sighed.

"You've had a long ride, I take it." When Cimarron nodded, Tess said, "Then you deserve a rest. I have a room over in the hotel with a feather bed and a goose-down pillow on it. You're welcome to use it—and me, if you're not *too* tired."

"Much obliged. I haven't had such a generous offer from such a good-looking lady in so long I'm outright overwhelmed."

"Well?"

"I'm sorry, Tess. I got business to see to."

"Won't it wait?"

"Nope."

"I won't either. Nice to have met you, cowboy."

Tess quickly emptied her glass and walked away from Cimarron.

He watched her go with mild regret. But who could tell? The world was a small one, and as big as the territory was, it wasn't unlikely that he'd find himself back in Claremore one day and then maybe he and Tess could share more than a drink together.

He paid the bartender and left the saloon.

He located the hotel Tess had mentioned, which turned out to be a sorry-looking two-story affair, and rented a room for the night.

After stripping off his clothes, he lay down on the room's bed and shifted about on the lumpy mattress beneath his back. As sleep ambushed him, he was thinking of Lila, having already almost forgotten Tess's name.

Tulsey Town, Cimarron discovered late the next afternoon, was a thriving city compared to either Claremore or Catoosa. Its streets were filled with wagons and people of all descriptions. Its hotel had a large and elaborate false front. Its residents thronged in and out of its many shops and stores.

Cimarron headed for the livery stable only minutes after arriving in the town and there, after sliding his Winchester from the boot, he turned his dun over to a beefy man with a florid face.

"I want him grain-fed," he told the man, stroking the dun's flank. "He's been eating so much grass I've been expecting him to turn into a sheep. Rub him down real good and curry him. And I'd be obliged to you if you'd wash out my saddle blanket and hang it up to dry."

As Cimarron left the livery stable, he decided to try the hotel first, partly because it was diagonally across the street from the livery and partly because hotels in a town like this one were often good sources of information. They were likely to have news not only about the town and the people in it, but also about what was going on in the surrounding countryside, as a result of people passing through and telling their tales, not all of them tall, some of them mostly truth.

"Yes, sir?" said the desk clerk as Cimarron walked across the lobby toward him. "Can I help you?"

"You can rent me a room."

"Glad to do that, sir." The clerk produced a worn ledger and pushed it toward Cimarron.

Cimarron registered and the clerk drew the ledger toward him. He glanced at what Cimarron had written and then up at Cimarron.

"Something wrong?" Cimarron asked.

"Oh, no, sir. It's just that Cimarron is—well, an unusual name."

"Well, maybe that means that I'm an unusual man. You can never tell."

The clerk took a key from a rack behind him and handed it to Cimarron. "Your room is on the second floor. I'm sure you'll have no difficulty finding it."

"I hope I don't have any difficulty locating a lady I'm looking for. A lady named Mrs. Reed. Mrs. Myra Belle Reed."

The clerk nervously licked his lips and ran a hand through his thinning hair.

"You know the lady?" Cimarron asked.

"Yes, sir. She is a guest of the hotel."

Well, now, Cimarron thought, pleased. Easy as eating a pickle on a toothpick. "What room's she in?"

"Fifteen. But—"

Cimarron left the desk and headed for the stairs, which

he quickly mounted, and then walked down the hall, his eyes on the numbers painted on the doors.

When he reached number fifteen, he halted and rapped on the door. He waited a moment and then rapped again, more loudly this time.

No one answered the door.

He looked down at the key in his hand, which bore a grimy tag attached to it by a piece of string. On the tag was penciled the number ten. He backtrailed, unlocked the door of number ten, and went inside.

He leaned his rifle against the wall, took off his hat, and then poured water from the pitcher in the porcelain bowl beside it. He washed his face and hands and then stripped off his shirt and bandanna and washed the upper half of his body.

The clerk, he thought as he scrubbed himself with the hotel's yellow soap, didn't look real happy when I asked about Mrs. Reed. He glanced in the mirror as he began to dry himself with a small towel. No wonder. With a face like mine, he probably thought I was one of her boys. Whatever the reason, he thought, the clerk looked like he had been about to piss in his pants when I mentioned Myra Belle.

One of her boys, he thought. Yep. That's the way I intend to play this hand. By becoming one of Myra Belle's boys. Just long enough to find out who killed Archie Kane. To find out if Sam Starr was really Kane's killer. Once he did find out—and if it did turn out to be Starr, as he believed it would—he'd take the man back to Fort Smith. With a stop at Lila's cabin first, of course.

"Of course," he said out loud, and smiled at his face in the mirror, which smiled brightly back at him.

He dressed, clapped his hat on his head, and then left the room, locking the door behind him.

He went downstairs and into the hotel's dining room, which was decorated with several potted plants that had seen better days and a few dusty paintings hanging on the walls.

He sat down at a table just inside the door, and a moment later, when a waiter appeared and handed him a handwritten menu, he scanned it and ordered ham, eggs, fried potatoes, boiled tomatoes, and coffee.

When the waiter had gone, Cimarron surveyed the room. There was a nice-looking young woman seated on the far side of the room. There was a nice-looking gold band on the ring finger of her left hand.

There were a couple of men at a nearby table in checkered suits going over a brand book. Stockmen, undoubtedly. A sprinkling of men who might be cowboys. Or bootleggers. It was hard to tell the difference in the territory.

When his food arrived, Cimarron began to devour it, hardly looking up from his plate as he did so. But he did catch a glimpse of the desk clerk, who suddenly appeared in the entrance to the dining room.

The clerk was pointing. At him.

A woman appeared beside the clerk. Her eyes were on Cimarron.

The clerk disappeared.

The woman came up to Cimarron's table and stood there, looking down at him as he continued to eat.

"Do you always eat with your hat on?" she asked him.

When he didn't reply, she said, "Such behavior shows a decided lack of civilized manners."

"Such behavior also shows how hungry a man happens to be." He took off his hat and plopped it down on the table. "The clerk told you I was looking for you, I take it."

"He did."

"Why don't you take yourself a seat, Mrs. Reed?"

Cimarron pushed his empty plate away from him as she sat down across from him and studied her.

She was almost as tall as he was and about as slender. But she wasn't at all slender in the places where a woman had no business being slender. Her breasts were full and pressed firmly against the scarlet bodice of her dress, which was delicately trimmed with bright white lace. She wore no hat over her shimmering black hair, which was coiled and pinned in place on top of her head.

Her eyes were black and her skin had known wind and weather. But the few wrinkles at the corners of her eyes and mouth did not detract from her quiet attractiveness.

"Why were you looking for me?" she asked bluntly.

103

"I have a failing. I'm always looking for pretty women like yourself."

"And you know the names of those women, even though you have never met them."

"Not always. But in your particular case, well, you're what a man might call fairly famous."

"You're being gallant. You might have said infamous."

"It don't seem right to insult a good-looking woman like yourself."

"The desk clerk said you call yourself Cimarron."

"I do."

"That's not a name. It's practically an epithet."

"An epithet? It's more like a symbol, seems to me."

"You talk like an educated man."

"I'm not, if you mean did I ever sit myself down in some school and listen to some professor lecture me about the decline and fall of the Roman Empire. But I read whenever I get the chance. A man can find out all kinds of things in between the covers of a book." Cimarron leaned back in his chair and hooked his thumbs in his cartridge belt. "I wish somebody'd write a book about you."

"So you could learn all kinds of things about me?"

"That's right. Maybe somebody will write a book about you someday, considering how you've been going about making a name for yourself."

"Have I been making a name for myself?"

"I'd like to have a part in helping you to keep on doing that very thing, Mrs. Reed."

"Don't call me that. The Mrs. Reed part of my life is over."

"You want me to call you Myra?"

"Belle will do. Myra is so very dowdy, don't you think?"

"But you're not, not by a long shot."

She ignored the compliment. "Belle, on the other hand, makes one think of—oh, nice things. Rainbows. Fancy-dress balls. Candlelight."

"Your name—be it Myra or Belle or both—makes some people think of lawlessness."

"It's quite clear that you are familiar with my reputation. And you have said that you want to help me continue making my name known in the Nations. How do you propose to do that?"

"Any way you'd order me to. Thieving mostly, I expect. Like Dade Munrow did."

"What do you know about Dade?"

"I know the Hanging Judge's got him locked up in Fort Smith's jail for stealing horses."

"He won't be locked up there for long, I can assure you. I've made arrangements to see to it that Dade is set free."

"What arrangements might you have made?" Cimarron asked, suddenly intensely interested in what Belle was saying.

She rose and, looking down at him, haughtily declared, "I am a naturally suspicious woman, Cimarron. In my line of work, I have to be. I am particularly suspicious of a man like yourself who rides into town out of the blue and comes looking for me, and when he finds me, claims he wants to work for me."

"I do want to work for you."

"Good-bye, Cimarron. It has been a pleasure talking with you. I'm sorry that nothing came of our discussion."

As Belle swept out of the dining room, Cimarron followed her with his eyes, damning her and himself for failing to accomplish what he had set out to do.

When she disappeared, he summoned the waiter, paid his bill, put on his hat, and strode out into the hotel lobby.

Belle was nowhere in sight.

He considered going up to her room to try again, but rejected the idea. Belle had struck him as a strong-willed woman. No, he'd have to come up with something better than he already had if he were to be successful in changing her mind about giving him the chance to ride for her.

He left the hotel and stood outside, his eyes on the bank at the far end of the street. He smiled to himself. Maybe he should rob it. That ought to dampen down any suspicions Belle had concerning him. He shook his head. There had to be a way. He'd find it.

But during the next two days, he found no way out of his dilemma.

He saw Belle twice during those two days. Each time

he spoke to her. Each time she politely acknowledged his greeting, but that was all.

On the third day after his arrival in Tulsey Town, he was just finishing his breakfast in the hotel dining room when loud voices on the far side of the room attracted his attention.

Two men seated at a table across the room were arguing heatedly.

The younger of the pair wore rough trail clothes; the older man wore a gray suit and gleaming white shirt.

As Cimarron watched the developing fracas, he saw the younger man suddenly rise, turn in his direction, and seize his companion by the throat with both hands.

The older man calmly reached behind him and slid his right hand under his coat. When the man's hand emerged from beneath his coat, there was a Remington Elliott .22 in his hand, which he had evidently retrieved from his waistband.

The younger man abruptly released his hold on the armed man's throat and stumbled backward, reaching for the revolver that was in the holster on his hip.

The older man barked an order and the would-be throttler threw his hands up into the air.

But then he quickly turned to make a run for it—and fell over his chair.

Cimarron leaped to his feet and swiftly circled the dining room. As he came up behind the man with the .22, he drew his Colt and said, "Drop it. That whore's gun in your hand's not accurate beyond a foot or two, and should you fire it, you're likely to kill anybody but the man you're aiming it at."

The man visibly stiffened and then started to turn toward Cimarron as his attacker got to his feet.

"You heard me tell you to drop that gun," Cimarron said, his voice cold. "Now you do it or I'll drop you right in your tracks."

The man placed the gun on the table.

"Pick it up," Cimarron said to the man who had been the gun's intended target, "and put it away."

When the man had done so, Cimarron said, "Now we can all go back to minding our own business."

"I wish," snapped the man with his back to Cimarron "that you'd minded yours right from the start."

"Howdy, Tucson," Cimarron said to the man who was standing on the other side of the table.

The man gave Cimarron a searching look. "By God, it's *you!*" he declared a moment later, astonishment on his face.

Cimarron put a finger to his lips and the man he had called Tucson fell silent. He spoke to the man he had disarmed. "Mister, my friend and me want to have a private conversation. You mind moving on?"

Muttering, the older man stalked from the dining room.

Tucson exuberantly called Cimarron by the name that Cimarron had not used or heard spoken in years.

"Tucson, you always were a loudmouthed son of a bitch. I don't use that name anymore and I don't want you to use it either. Now I'm called Cimarron. You got that? Cimarron."

"I got it," Tucson said, grinning and resuming his seat at the table. "Where the hell have you been hiding all this time, Cimarron? I haven't seen you in—what is it, two years now?"

As Cimarron sat down at the table, he answered, "Three."

"Well, I want to thank you for what you just did for me."

"You're welcome, old son. When I recognized you, I thought I ought to come to the aid of an old friend, so I up and did."

"That drummer was daft," Tucson announced. "Claims I struck up a conversation with him out in the lobby just so I could steal his watch."

Cimarron leaned back in his chair. "What time is it, Tucson?"

Tucson pulled a thin gold watch from his hatband, opened it, and said, "Twelve past seven."

"Still up to your old tricks, I see."

Tucson cast a shifty glance around the dining room and shoved the watch into his pocket. "He almost had me dead to rights, that drummer did. He didn't feel me lift his watch, but then he went looking for it here at the table and that's when he caught on."

"What're you doing to occupy your time these days, Tucson?"

"Got a regular riding job now, Cimarron."

"Who're you riding for?"

"Well, I hate to admit it but I'm riding for a woman." Tucson blushed.

"You don't mean Myra Belle Reed, do you?"

"I do. You know Belle, Cimarron?"

"We've met."

"Belle's a real lady. Even though she does her share of carousing and occasional fornicating." Tucson winked at Cimarron. "But where've you been, Cimarron? And why the hell did you disappear the way you did that day down in Texas? I remember we were robbing that bank and everything was going along real smooth until that sheriff dropped in on us and you killed him with your first shot."

Cimarron was silent, listening to the ghost of his father closing in on him again.

"Why'd you go and ride off like you did that day, Cimarron? You even left your share of the loot behind. You never said so much as a single word to any of us. You just went and rode off, and none of us ever saw you again."

"Would you take it amiss if I didn't try to explain to you why I rode off that day like I did?" *Explain to you that the sheriff I shot to death turned out to be my father?*

"I'm not quick to take offense," Tucson declared. "You had your reasons, I guess, and that's good enough for me. You know something, Cimarron? I'm so damned glad to see you again, I could do a dance on a dime. You were the best friend I ever had."

"We were close as two peas in a pod, all right," Cimarron agreed, and then gritted his teeth as the ghost of his father caught up with him, gave him a sorrowful look, and moved slowly on.

"What've you been doing since I last saw you, Cimarron?"

"Drifting."

"You doing all right?"

Cimarron seized the opportunity he had been waiting for. "Nope. Down on my luck, I am, Tucson, if the truth's to be told. If something doesn't turn up real soon, I'm in big trouble, looks like."

"I'll bet you're still good with a gun."

"I am."

"That reminds me. I not only got that drummer's watch but I also got his belly gun, thanks to you." Tucson picked it up and then reached across the table and playfully punched Cimarron's arm. "I got an idea."

Cimarron raised his eyebrows questioningly.

"Belle's always in the market for hands that can do her kind of work. *You* could do it, Cimarron."

"Well, I've heard about Belle and the Reed gang. And you know I've had a lot of experience doing the kind of work her boys do."

"Sure, you have. You were one real bad outlaw in the old days. Tell you what. Let's go see Belle. She lives here in the hotel at the moment. I'll be mighty proud to introduce you to her as a good friend of mine and to tell her you and me used to ride together."

"Maybe we'll get a chance to ride together again if the lady's amenable once you've vouched for me."

"I sure hope so," Tucson said sincerely.

So do I, Cimarron thought.

8

Belle opened her hotel-room door only a moment after Tucson had knocked on it.

She showed no surprise when she saw Cimarron standing in the hall beside Tucson.

"Belle," Tucson began, "this here's a good friend of mine named Cimarron. He said you two had met. Could we come in and have a talk with you?"

Belle stepped aside, and after Cimarron and Tucson had entered her room, she closed the door behind them. "What do you want to talk about?" she asked Tucson, but her wary eyes were on Cimarron.

Cimarron's eyes were on the shirtless and bootless man lounging on the unmade bed near the window.

Tucson replied, "Cimarron wants to join up with us."

Belle's hard eyes remained on Cimarron.

The man on the bed spoke then. "Tucson, get him out of here. He's just a drifter, by the looks of him. Besides, we don't need any more men."

"Cimarron," Tucson said, "this here's Sam Starr." He gestured to the man on the bed who had just spoken. "Sam, this friend of mine might be a drifter, but he's also one or two other things you and Belle ought to know about. For one thing, him and me rode with a gang of hard cases down in Texas and we did all right for ourselves. For another thing, Cimarron's good with a gun—real good."

As Tucson went on to explain about the day the gang of which Cimarron had been a member had robbed the bank in Texas and how Cimarron had killed the sheriff who had come into the bank in the middle of the robbery with his gun drawn, Cimarron briefly closed his eyes, then opened them, and steeled himself to continue listening to what Tucson was saying.

"So what I'm saying is Cimarron'd be an asset to us," Tucson concluded.

"How long have you known this drifter?" Starr asked him.

"We rode together for more than a year all told," Tucson answered.

Belle commented, "It does seem, Cimarron, if Tucson is telling the truth—"

"Belle, you know I'm no liar," Tucson interrupted. "At least, not about something as important as this."

"It seems," Belle continued, unperturbed by the interruption, "that Cimarron has the credentials for the kind of job we can offer him, Sam."

"Sure he has!" Tucson declared enthusiastically, and slapped Cimarron's shoulder. "He's got more credentials than a cur's got fleas!"

"You're the boss, Belle," Starr said as he pulled on his boots and then his shirt.

Cimarron studied the man. He saw a dark face with prominent cheekbones, thin, almost-nonexistent lips. Starr's straight black hair practically covered his broad forehead. His ears hugged the sides of his head and his hooked nose had wide, flaring nostrils. He looked to Cimarron to be exactly what Lila had called him—a Cherokee bandit.

"All right," Belle said firmly, "I'll give you a chance if you want it, Cimarron."

When Cimarron remained silent, Tucson nudged him in the ribs.

"What? Oh, sure, a chance. Much obliged, Belle. That's real nice of you. What kind of a chance?"

Belle seated herself in a wicker chair that stood in front of the window. The light streaming through the window behind her haloed her head and the shadows it cast hid her features.

She folded her hands in her lap and said, "I have a very solid and lucrative operation going here, Cimarron. I took it over when my husband, Jim, was killed by Sheriff Morris two years ago. I run the Reed gang now and I

111

want that clearly understood. I give the orders. You, Tucson, Sam—all of you follow them.

"Whether you last with me, Cimarron, depends on whether you can follow my orders and upon whether you can do what you're told to do. If you don't or can't, you're out. And out means dead, since we don't want any strays wandering around with information about me and my boys that could be damaging to us in a court of law."

"*Whooeeee!*" Tucson whooped. He grabbed Cimarron's hand and shook it vigorously. "You're in!" he yelped happily.

"But you'll be out," Belle warned, "the first time you fail me."

"I wouldn't dare fail a woman like you, Belle," Cimarron said quietly.

Their eyes locked.

Starr muttered something and stood up, heading for the door.

As he opened it, Belle said, "Tucson, I won't be needing you for anything."

Tucson turned and followed Starr out into the hall.

As Cimarron started for the door, Belle said, "Not you, Cimarron. You stay."

When the door closed behind Tucson and Starr, Belle said, "Sit down, Cimarron."

There was, he noted, only one chair in the room and Belle occupied it. He glanced at the unmade bed.

"Sit down," Belle repeated.

He crossed the room and sat down on the bed.

"When we first met, you said you knew my reputation," Belle began. "Exactly what do you know about me?"

"That you run this outfit, like you just said."

"Did you know that I have two children?"

"Nope."

"I have. Pearl was my first. Her daddy was one of the most wonderful men I ever knew. His name was Cole Younger."

"Heard of him. Him and his three brothers rode with Frank and Jesse James, I heard."

Belle nodded. "I'll never see Cole again. Did you know

112

that he and his brother, Bob, are in Stillwater State Prison?"

It was Cimarron's turn to nod.

"When little Pearl was born," Belle continued, "I left her with my parents, and because polite Texas society scorned me because of the scandal—Pearl was a love child—I went to Dallas and learned to take care of myself."

"You do strike me as a woman who can take care of herself, all right."

"That's why I'm telling you all this. I want you to understand me and what I expect of you." Belle paused a moment. "In Dallas, I sang in dance halls and I became a very proficient dealer. I dealt monte, faro, poker. I'm not unintelligent. I have a stiff backbone and a sharp tongue, as you'll undoubtedly learn sooner or later. There's not a man been born yet can best me at anything I set out to do."

"I believe it."

"One day, I met Jim Reed and I fell in love with him." Belle's eyes, which had been gazing into space, flicked toward Cimarron and then away. "Jim had sandy hair and a wonderful Roman nose. He was tall and slender. We married and I had a little boy—Edward. That was in California. But things got hot for us there, so we came here. Then, two years ago, Sheriff Morris killed Jim. Since then, I've been running things, and running them well. Jim and I used to hide out on old Tom Starr's ranch. You just met one of Tom's sons—Sam. Full bloods, the Starrs. I intend to marry Sam Starr."

"He's a handsome enough fellow."

"Isn't he?" The faint trace of a smile drifted across Belle's face. It was gone when she added, "When I become Belle Starr I will also acquire dower rights to the Starr ranch, which is in the bend of the Canadian River just below Hi-Early Mountain."

Cimarron said nothing, but he could not help admiring Belle. She didn't fumble her way through life the way many people did. Not Belle. It was apparent to him that she scouted the land around her and made her plans carefully. All in all, she was a woman to be reckoned with. He'd have to step lively to keep at least one step ahead of

113

her. He wondered what she would do if she found out that he was a lawman. He thought he knew, and what he thought chilled him.

"I take care of my boys," Belle said. "If you get into any trouble with the law, I assure you that you can count on me to get you the best lawyer available. I've gotten more men out from under Judge Parker's thumb than I can recall at the moment. And at this very moment, I'm in the process of getting another one out, as I mentioned to you the first time we met."

"Dade Munrow?" Cimarron was careful to betray none of the excitement he had begun to feel.

"I've got a man out after the only witness who can get Dade convicted of that horse-stealing charge Parker's planning to try him on. Once Archie Kane is out of the way, they'll either release Dade for lack of evidence against him or try him and watch their case against him collapse around their ears with Kane dead and unable to testify against Dade." Belle patted her hair and said, "But Cory should have been back here by now and he's not. That worries me."

"Maybe he couldn't find Kane," Cimarron suggested, his thoughts racing.

"Kane should have been easy to find. Dade and Kane both rode for me. We all know where Kane's cabin is in Creek Nation. What worries me is the fact that Kane might have gotten the drop on Cory."

As Belle fell silent, her face pensive, Cimarron saw his theory concerning what Kane had told him—had tried to tell him just before he died—collapse.

He had believed that Sam Starr might have been the one who had gunned Kane down because Kane had pointed to the sky—to the stars in it.

Even when Cimarron, after entering the room where he now sat, had found out that Starr was the man on the bed, he had believed that Starr might have killed Kane and returned to Tulsey Town. But now Belle had told him that a man named Cory had been sent gunning for Kane.

Since he knew that Kane was dead, he was left, as Belle was, with a question: Where was Cory?

"To hell with Cory," Belle said suddenly and sharply.

"We've got more important things to worry about than where Cory is at the moment."

"Like what?"

"Elias Hall."

"Who's Elias Hall?"

"He used to be a chief of one of the Creek towns—Chiaha Town. He was also a very industrious man in his younger days. In the late thirties, he went into competition with the private contractors who were supplying the army with provisions to feed the Creeks after the Removal. He hired white men to run his operation and it was a long time before anyone knew Hall was behind the operation.

"He steamboated things like pork, flour, and salt up from New Orleans to Fort Coffee to sell to the army for distribution to the Indians. He had his people sell their produce and livestock to the wives of the officers and soldiers garrisoned at Fort Gibson.

"He made a great deal of money, it's rumored. And he was not what you could call a profligate man. He kept most of his money or reinvested it in his various enterprises."

As Belle broke into a smile, Cimarron said, "We're going to take his money away from Elias Hall, is that it?"

"It is and we are. He lives due west of here. It's about a thirty-mile ride. You, Sam, and Tucson will go there and you will make Hall tell you where he has his money hidden. When he does tell you, you'll get it and bring it back here to me."

"How much money do you figure Hall has?"

"Rumor has it that he's stored away—somewhere—as much as twenty thousand dollars."

Cimarron let out a low whistle.

The sun was setting as Cimarron rode west with Starr and Tucson.

"Like old times, isn't it?" Tucson, who was riding beside Cimarron, remarked.

"Sure is," Cimarron said, remembering the years he had tried so hard to forget.

"Hall's son's got two wives," Starr commented laconically. "They say they're comely."

"Even if they're not," Tucson said, grinning, "that's real good news. I haven't had me a woman in a week."

"Sounds like we have a crowd to contend with," Cimarron observed.

"There's Elias Hall," Starr said, "and his son, Artus. Artus' two wives—Molly and Beatrice. But we shouldn't have much trouble. The old man's so old he hasn't got the strength to so much as spit. We can handle the two women easy. Artus might put up a fight. But there's three of us and only one of him."

They rode on in silence for several miles until Tucson suddenly pointed off into the gathering gloom and said, "There's some kind of shindig up ahead."

Cimarron's eyes were on the huge bonfire blazing in the distance, a darting red eye in the young night. Figures were occasionally silhouetted against it. He judged the fire to be almost a mile away.

"We'll move off to the south," Starr said. "There's no point in letting those Creeks up there see us. They might remember us and start thinking we had something to do with what's going to happen to the Hall family."

Cimarron turned his horse and followed Starr south, Tucson riding behind him.

Again the three men rode in silence for some time, leaving the bonfire and the Creeks who had been clustered around it far behind them.

Later, when a dim light became visible in the distance, Starr said, "That's the Hall cabin. We'll leave our horses over there in the trees and go in on foot."

After Cimarron had tethered his dun to a poplar, he followed Starr and Tucson as the pair made their way stealthily toward the large cabin from which the dim light was shining through the chinks in a shuttered window.

By the light of the moon Cimarron was able to make out the chimney on the right wall of the cabin. It was made of stone that reached halfway up the side of the cabin wall. Above the stonework, sticks that had been daubed with mud completed the chimney. He could make out a garden on the left side of the cabin that was bordered by a small grove of peach trees. Also visible near the cabin was a cow pen and a log pen covered with thatch that evidently served the Halls as a stable. The cabin itself had a pole roof that held split oak shingles in place.

Starr held up a hand and they all halted, listening.

No sound came from inside the cabin.

"They must be still up and about," Starr said in a low voice. "If they weren't, there wouldn't be a light." He stepped up to the cabin door, drew his revolver, and reached for the wooden latch. Swiftly he pulled the door open.

Light from a coal oil lamp on a table inside the cabin spilled across the threshold.

A woman who had been seated at the table leaped to her feet and took a backward step, her hand rising to cover her mouth.

"Don't you move!" Starr ordered her as he stepped inside the cabin, followed by Cimarron and Tucson. "Where's everybody?"

Cimarron took in the room in one swift glance. It contained hand-hewn wooden furniture that was held together by wooden pegs. On the room's right wall a rifle hung on wooden hooks. A few shelves that held blankets, woven baskets, candles, and an array of wooden bowls and utensils lined the walls. There was a puncheon floor beneath Cimarron's feet.

"I asked you a question, woman," Starr growled.

"They're not here," she answered. "I mean, my father-in-law is here. I agreed to stay with him while my husband and his other wife went to the busk."

"To the what?" Tucson asked, frowning.

"We happened on the busk back along the trail," Cimarron told him. "It's a kind of get-together held by the Creeks."

"That's right," the woman said, and pointed to a length of hemlock lying on the table beside the lamp.

"What are you getting at?" Starr asked her, his eyes on the stick.

"Today was the day when everyone was to go to the busk," the woman replied. "There was just one stick left from the bundle."

Starr started to speak, but Cimarron spoke first. "You've scared the daylights out of the lady, Starr. What she's trying to tell you is it's Creek practice to give a

117

bundle of sticks to each family to help them keep track of the days before a big meeting like the busk. Each day the family tosses away one stick in the bundle. When there's but one left, well, that means the big day's at hand."

"My husband went to the busk," the woman said nervously. "But my father-in-law couldn't. Elias is sickly, you see. I— What do you men want here?"

"Shut up!" Starr snapped. "Tucson, take a look around back. Cimarron, you search the cabin to make sure this lady's telling us the truth."

As Tucson turned and went outside, Cimarron took a candle from one of the wall shelves, lit it from the lamp, and went down the passageway, which he found connected the two large rooms at each of its ends.

He entered the room at the end of the passageway, and by the light of the candle he was able to make out the shriveled form of an old man sleeping on one of the beds in the room, all of which were made of poles driven into holes that had been bored in the cabin's wall. The beds had supports at their opposite ends.

"Chief Hall," Cimarron said tentatively.

The old man stirred and then blinked up at Cimarron. "I don't know you," he said querulously in a cracked voice. "Do I know you?"

"You're alone here tonight with your son's wife?"

"I don't know. Maybe I am. I've been asleep."

Cimarron left the room and returned to the one in which Starr was waiting for him. "The old man's in the room at the end of the passageway," he told Starr.

Tucson reentered the room and said, "Everything's quiet outside. There's no sign of anybody." He glanced at the woman, who now stood with her back pressed up against the wall. "What's your name, missy?"

"Molly."

Tucson crossed the room and put an arm around her waist. "Pretty little thing, now, aren't you just?"

Cimarron watched as Molly struggled to free herself from Tucson's grip. She was a small woman. No more than thirty, he guessed. Her long black hair hung down her back and there was fear in her equally black eyes as she struggled to free herself of Tucson's grip. Her hips flared gracefully below her waist and above it her small

118

breasts were pressed against Tucson's broad chest. The skin of her face and hands was the color of bare earth with the sun blazing down upon it.

"Let her go!" Starr ordered Tucson, and when Tucson had released Molly, Starr ordered her to go and get her father-in-law and bring him back with her.

Cimarron stepped to one side to let her pass.

"Go with her, Tucson," Starr ordered. "There might be some way for her to get out of that other room."

"There isn't," Tucson declared confidently. "I checked."

Starr gestured with his gun. "Go with her."

Tucson went.

"What do you think, Starr?" Cimarron asked when Tucson had disappeared down the passageway.

"About what?"

"Look at this place. Handmade chairs and table. Only a hatchet was used to make this stuff. These walls are chinked with only mud to keep the wind out. Those bowls and things on the shelves—simple stuff. This doesn't look to me like the home of a man who's got twenty thousand dollars hid somewheres."

"Most Creek farmers have little more than a one-room cabin," Starr countered. "But Hall's got what amounts to two cabins connected to each other. His son's got two wives. Creek tribal law allows a man to have two—or more—wives only if he can afford to keep them."

"You're going to try to make the old man tell you if he's got any money hid hereabouts?"

"If he won't talk, maybe that Molly will." Starr winked at Cimarron.

Cimarron's face remained expressionless as he realized what he'd gotten himself into. He didn't like the look he saw in Starr's eyes. He had seen that look before in the eyes of men with a taste for cruelty. It was a hot look born of the dark and dangerous fires that burned within such men.

Some lawman I'm turning out to be, he thought. I've got myself right in the middle of what's likely to turn out to be a downright mean type of lawlessness.

"Please!"

Molly's voice caused Cimarron to turn around.

119

Tucson was gripping her left arm and roughly shoving her ahead of him as they made their way along the passageway. Behind them, dressed only in a long cotton nightshirt, came Elias Hall, holding on to the wall for support.

Tucson forced Molly to sit down in a chair he pulled out from the table.

"Come on in here, Hall," Starr called out to the blinking Creek as he fumbled his way along the passageway.

"Who are all these men?" Hall asked Molly, his voice petulant. "What are they doing here? Where is Artus? Why isn't my son here?"

"Hush, Elias," Molly whispered to the old man. She got up from her chair and went to him. After helping him to seat himself at the table, she sat down again in the chair in which Tucson had placed her earlier.

"We hear you're a rich man," Starr said, staring down at Hall.

"Rich in years," Hall muttered without looking up.

"You're rich in money too," Starr snapped. "Now we want to know where you keep your money."

"I have no money," Hall retorted angrily. "I'm a poor man and I live a simple life."

Starr's fisted right hand shot out and struck Hall on the side of the head.

The old man let out a mournful wail and began to weep.

"Don't!" Molly cried, and ran to him. She took up a position between Hall and Starr.

"I won't hit him again," Starr told her almost sweetly. "Not if he turns over his money to us, I won't."

"I have no money," Hall cried, his cheeks wet with his tears. "Please—you men—you go away from here and leave us alone!"

Starr reached out and seized Molly's arm. He pulled her toward him and at the same time reached out with his free hand and struck Hall another blow, which sent the man toppling from his chair.

"Stop it!" Molly screamed, trying to break free of Starr. "He'll never tell you where the money is!"

"So there *is* money!" Starr exulted. "I knew there

120

was!" He reached for Hall, who was whimpering wordlessly.

"I'd tell you where it is," Molly said quickly. "But I honestly don't know. The only person Elias ever told about where he had hidden his money was his son—my husband. But Artus has never told anyone else. Not me. No one! That's the truth! You must believe me!"

"Tucson, take her." Starr shoved Molly away from him.

Tucson caught her. His arms encircled her.

Cimarron gritted his teeth. She's gone and done it, he thought. If only she'd kept quiet about the money, Starr, he believed, would have begun to doubt that there was any money to be stolen from Hall. But by speaking as she had, Molly had not saved the old man, as she had evidently hoped to do, but placed him in even greater danger—along with herself—despite her claim of having no knowledge of where the money was hidden.

"That feels real good," Tucson said, and laughed as Molly, with her back pressed against him, struggled to free herself. "You just keep rubbing up against me like that and the first thing you know I'll be in love with you—at least that long part of me I've got between my legs will be."

Starr seized Hall and dragged him to his feet. He held him in both hands and shook him.

Hall's head bobbed back and forth. His wails filled the room.

Starr released him, raised a booted foot, and kicked the old man, sending him crashing into the wall.

As Hall slumped to the floor, looking like a broken bag of bones, his eyes closed.

Cimarron saw them glaze. "You've killed him, Starr."

Starr went to where the old man lay and shook him. When Hall did not respond, he repeated his action. Hall hung limp in his hands. Starr swore and let him fall to the floor.

Molly screamed, a high shrill sound in the suddenly quiet room.

Starr turned around and stared at her. "It's your turn now," he almost purred, the lamplight glistening in his dark eyes.

121

"No," Molly murmured. "Oh, no!"

As Starr moved toward her, Cimarron stepped between them. "Hold it, Starr."

Starr's eyes flashed. "What the hell are you talking about?"

"I'm talking about playing your last ace. You kill her, you're completely out of luck."

"I won't kill her. Hurt her some, that's all. Till she talks."

"There's a better way of using her," Cimarron said, his voice low and steady.

"I know what that way is," Tucson cried. "We can take turns!"

Cimarron ignored the outburst. "Starr, her husband knows where the money is."

"But he's not here. She is."

"Artus Hall is at the busk," Cimarron reminded Starr. "It's him who can tell us what we want to know. Molly might also know, but then again she might not. You might just be wasting your time with her."

Starr glanced at Molly and then back at Cimarron. "She might have lied before. She might damn well know where the money's hid."

"It's possible," Cimarron admitted. "But I'm a man who likes to bet on a sure thing. Artus Hall looks to me like a sure thing. Molly, she's doubtful. And time's a-wasting."

Starr hesitated.

Tucson said, "I'm hungry as hell."

"I know what you're hungry for," Starr muttered.

"No, this time I'm hungry for some food. The other can come along later." Tucson's hand came to rest on Molly's breast.

Cimarron watched it move roughly over the material of Molly's dress and then slide beneath the striped calico. "Well, Starr?"

"Go get the old man's son. But don't give our game away. Tell him we got his wife and father. Don't tell him the old man's dead. Bring him back here and then I'll go to work on him just like I did on his daddy."

Cimarron turned and started for the door.

Tucson called his name.

As Cimarron turned around, Tucson ripped Molly's bodice. He held out a piece of cloth he had torn from it, leaving Molly's left breast bare. "Take this with you, Cimarron. Her husband might want some proof that what you'll be telling him is true."

Then he licked his lips greedily and quickly put his mouth to Molly's nipple, his hand over her own mouth to keep her from screaming.

Cimarron, knowing he could do nothing to stop Molly's violation, took the torn piece of calico, pocketed it, and left the cabin.

9

When Cimarron arrived at the open area where the busk was being held, the festivities were still in progress.

He halted his horse just beyond the light that was thrown by the huge bonfire, and studied the scene before him.

In the distance, a ball game was being played by nearly a score of young men. Many of them were shirtless and the sweat on their bodies gleamed in the light of the fire.

They held long hickory sticks in their hands with which they struck the stuffed rawhide ball and then they raced noisily after it, sometimes using their sticks to surreptitiously trip a competing player. The long black hair of several of the Creeks was plastered by sweat to their shoulders and bare backs.

Cimarron heeled his dun and rode slowly toward the fire, halting the horse not far from it, near a group of men who were watching the ball game and enthusiastically betting on its outcome.

The *thwump* of hickory sticks against the ball blended with the thudding sound of bare feet striking the earth as the women weaved and bowed in the intricate patterns of a dance that had no musical accompaniment.

"Can anybody tell me where I might find Mr. or Mrs. Hall?" Cimarron asked, and the men in the small crowd turned to stare up at him.

No one spoke at first, but then a man detached himself from the group and walked up to Cimarron. "May I ask if you are a friend of Artus Hall and his wife?"

"I've got a message to give him," Cimarron replied, dodging the question. "It's real important."

"I saw Artus earlier," the man said, glancing around at

the men playing ball and the women intently dancing. "I'm afraid, though, that I don't see him at the moment."

"What about his wife? You see her anywhere?" Cimarron was careful to keep the growing sense of impatience he was feeling out of his voice in order to avoid arousing any suspicion or, worse, alarm.

The man shook his head. Turning to Cimarron, he said, "I'm sorry but I don't see her anywhere."

"Then I'd best mosey on and see if I can find someone who's seen them."

"Perhaps you would like to join our young men in their ball game," the man suggested. "Artus or Beatrice are bound to put in an appearance sooner or later."

It better be sooner, Cimarron thought. "No, thanks," he said, declining the invitation. "I might get my ribs busted before I got anywhere near that ball your boys out there are slamming around."

"Some of the men will soon join the women in their dancing. Perhaps—"

Cimarron shook his head. "I could never master the pattern of those steps. They're far too tricky for me."

"The steps are intricate. Some of them take years to learn properly and even longer to fully master."

"No wonder you Creeks claim that the bears taught you your dances one day long ago. And you want to know something? I think you're right in believing that. Like you people claim, no mere man or woman could have invented such in-and-out stepping and roundabout sashaying."

Cimarron was about to ride away when a woman came running up to the man to whom he had been speaking, a large wooden bowl and a feather in her hands.

"Martin," she said breathlessly, "I've brought you some of the black drink." She handed the bowl and the feather to the man she had called Martin.

He took it from her and offered it to Cimarron. "We Creeks are happy to share with strangers. Will you drink the black drink with me and my wife?"

Cimarron hesitated briefly and then took the bowl and feather that Martin handed him. "What is this, if I may be so bold as to ask?"

"Assi-luputski," Martin answered.

"I don't talk your language. What's assi—what did you call this?"

"*Assi-luputski*," Martin repeated with a smile. "It is the Creek word for what in English is often called simply the black drink. Its color results from boiling leaves of ilex cassine in water together with various roots and herbs. It's a cure for many ailments, or so we Creeks claim." He leaned toward Cimarron and whispered, "But any emetic like this one would cure whatever might ail a man. If it didn't kill him first." He laughed.

"This here's an emetic?" When Martin nodded, Cimarron said, "I think I'd rather not accept your hospitality, if you don't mind." He handed Martin the bowl and feather and watched him drink deeply.

And then begin to vomit violently.

The woman beside Martin watched his paroxysms with apparent pleasure, and when they had ended, she said, "Martin, we must soon go home. It's getting very late. But first, come down to the spring with me. Chief Raines is there and he's going to bless the water. I want you to drink some of it so you'll stay well. Then we must take some of the new fire and hurry home."

"Ruth," Martin said to his wife, "this stranger is looking for Artus and Beatrice Hall. Have you seen them?"

Ruth glanced shyly at Cimarron and replied, "They are down at the spring."

"Come with my wife and me," Martin said to Cimarron. "You can watch Chief Raines—he's what you would probably call our medicine man—bless the spring water while you deliver your message to the Halls. Unless, of course, you scorn what many white men call our savage superstitions."

"I don't scorn what another man believes. I've seen what yesterday was called magic turn out to be tomorrow's science. Take sulfur and molasses. My ma dosed me with it every spring when I was a boy. Some said it was worthless. But two years ago, a doctor fresh from Saint Louis told a friend of mine down in Texas to take it and it cured him of his complaint."

Martin laughed, took his wife's hand, and beckoned to Cimarron, who walked his horse behind the pair as they made their way to the small spring visible in the distance around which a crowd was gathering.

When they reached it, Martin said, "That's Chief Raines." He pointed to a swarthy man wearing a black vest over his gray shirt and striped woolen trousers.

Cimarron was not interested in Raines or in the chant the man was muttering as he held a reed in his right hand and people drew water from the spring in small bowls that they held out to him. Raines stopped chanting long enough to place one end of his reed into his mouth and the other end in the water contained in one of the bowls. He blew through the hollow reed into the water, causing it to bubble, and then resumed his chanting.

"Where are the Halls?" Cimarron asked abruptly, his voice rising above the sound of Raines' chanting.

"Over there," Martin said, pointing to a couple standing near Raines who were drinking from two small bowls filled with the spring water that Raines had just blessed.

"Much obliged." Cimarron got out of the saddle and led his dun over to the Halls. "Mr. Hall," he said, "I've got to talk to you."

Hall stared skeptically at Cimarron. "I don't know you."

"That's right. You don't. But like I said, I've got to talk to you and Mrs. Hall."

"Go ahead. Talk."

"Not here. Someplace private."

Beatrice Hall, the bowl in her hand forgotten, clutched her husband's arm. "Is something wrong, Artus?"

Hall's eyes narrowed as he asked Cimarron, "*Is* there something wrong?"

"Yes," Cimarron answered bluntly, "there surely is. Now you two and me had better talk. It's important. It's about your other wife, Mr. Hall. And your father."

"Artus!" Beatrice Hall exclaimed. "What is it?"

Hall shook his arm free of his wife and said, "We can go into the woods over there."

He led the way, Beatrice at his side, Cimarron following and leading his horse.

When they were beneath the trees, Hall said, "Now tell me what this is all about. Who are you?"

Cimarron ignored his second question. "There are two

men who're holding your wife back at your house. They've already killed your father and—"

Beatrice's shrill cry interrupted Cimarron.

"Quiet!" he said. "Keep quiet now, both of you."

"These two men," Hall said, shock twisting his features. "What do they want?"

"They came looking to steal the money your father's said to have hid. He wouldn't tell them where it is and they roughed him up—killed him. Your wife Molly claimed that you, Hall, are the only other person who knows where the money's at. I'm to take you back to your cabin and I can tell you you'd best turn over the money to them or they'll kill your wife same as they did your father."

"I don't believe you," Hall said. "How do I know you're telling the truth?"

Cimarron pulled the piece of calico from his pocket and handed it to Hall.

"That's from Molly's dress," Beatrice exclaimed. "I know it is!"

Hall looked from the piece of cloth in his hand to Cimarron's face. "What's your part in all this?"

"Never mind about that. Let's go."

Beatrice, her voice a whisper, said, "Artus, we can't go back there if this is true. Those men might kill us too."

"I've got to go back," Hall said firmly. "Because of what those men might do to Molly if I don't. You stay here, Beatrice."

"But, Artus, it might be a trap of some kind."

"It might be," Hall agreed, his eyes still on Cimarron's face. "But I can't take a chance that it isn't." He paused a moment and then started to speak, but Cimarron interrupted him.

"I see you're not armed, Hall. How many of the men here are carrying guns?"

"No man is," Hall answered. "We don't come armed to a busk."

Cimarron turned and looked back at the bonfire. At the women dancing. At the young men still playing ball.

No guns, he thought.

The tempo of the dancers suddenly increased.

There's no way out of this situation, he thought. Not if

128

I'm to save Molly Hall. Not if I'm not to give myself away to Starr and Tucson.

A hickory stick *thwacked* against the rawhide ball, which went sailing over the leaping flames of the bonfire.

As Cimarron watched it soar up and over them, an idea came to him.

"Listen to me, Hall," he said. "Here's what we're going to do to try to straighten out this mess your family's in."

As Cimarron and Hall rode up to Hall's cabin, Cimarron asked, "Now, you're sure you know what to do?"

"I know what to do," Hall responded glumly. "But what if your plan doesn't work?"

Cimarron started to speak, but then the cabin door burst open and a figure darted out into the night.

"Tucson?" Cimarron called out to whoever it was who had ducked into the shadows to the left of the door.

"Cimarron? That you?"

The voice that came out of the darkness wasn't Tucson's voice.

"Starr, I brought Hall."

As Cimarron and Hall dismounted, Starr stepped into the light. In his hand was his revolver.

"Take him inside," Starr said, his eyes on Hall.

As Cimarron gave Hall a shove that sent him careening through the open door, Starr moved in behind him.

Cimarron followed Starr into the cabin and closed the door. He was just in time to hear Hall's stricken cry.

"You killed him!" Hall cried, and spun around to face Starr, who was holding his revolver on him. "You killed my father!"

Hall seemed to be about to lunge at Starr, but then Starr raised his six-gun slightly and Hall began to quiver. He turned around and dropped to his knees on the puncheon floor. He cradled his dead father in his arms as tears appeared in his eyes and began to run down his cheeks. He failed to stifle his sobs, which racked his body.

So far, so good, Cimarron thought. He was pleased at the way Hall had displayed what had seemed like genuine surprise when he first saw his father lying dead on the floor. Cimarron had warned him to act surprised when he saw his father's body so that Starr wouldn't know that Hall had already been told that his father had been killed.

"You can get on with your mourning when we've got your old man's money," Starr told Hall. "Where is it?"

"My wife first," Hall said between clenched teeth. "I want to see my wife."

"Fair enough," Starr said. "Cimarron go get her. Her and Tucson, they're in the other cabin."

Cimarron went down the passageway, his boots thudding on the floor, and on into the room at its end. He halted just inside the door.

Molly, as naked as Tucson, was lying on the bed where he had first seen Elias Hall—beneath Tucson. Her face was turned toward the wall so Cimarron could not see it. Tucson's head was buried in the bedding as he continued thrusting himself into the motionless Molly, grunting, unaware of Cimarron's presence.

"Starr wants her," Cimarron said sharply.

Tucson's contorted face appeared from the tangle of bedding, but he didn't seem to recognize Cimarron. He continued his rapid, almost-frantic movements, his lips working wetly.

"In a minute," Cimarron heard him murmur. "In just a—" He dropped down upon Molly and a long low moan issued from his lips. He lay without moving for what seemed to Cimarron endless minutes. Then he stirred and withdrew from Molly, who still did not move or turn her head.

He suddenly yawned as if he were just waking up. "Whew, that was something! Even without the lady's cooperation. I feel like I could just about lick my weight in butterflies right now, and that's a fact."

Cimarron crossed the room and spoke softly to Molly. "Your husband's here. He wants to see you." He stood there helplessly, watching her weep silently, her arms at her sides, her face twisted in a terrible grimace. "Molly, you don't want anything to happen to your husband. Something bad might if you don't get up and come with me."

Tucson, as he rose from the bed and began to dress, said, "Starr went first. He claimed it was his privilege as

130

the boss of this operation. You're welcome to her, Cimarron, if you don't mind being third in line."

"Get the hell out of here!"

When Tucson started to protest, Cimarron ordered. He said, "I brought Hall back. He's out there with Starr. You'd better go see if Starr wants you for anything."

Moments later, grumbling to himself, Tucson left the room.

Cimarron bent over and picked up Molly's clothes, which had been lying in a pile beside the bed. Then, leaning over, he said, "Here's your clothes. Put them on. I'll wait for you out in the passageway."

He dropped her clothes on the bed and left the room.

Several minutes later, Starr shouted his name as he stood waiting for Molly in the passageway.

"Be right there," he yelled back, and turned to find Molly standing behind him wearing her torn dress.

Her face was impassive and her arms hung listlessly at her sides.

Cimarron reached out to take her hand. She rapidly recoiled from him as if he had been about to strike her. He withdrew his hand and said, "Come on. Follow me. Your husband's waiting for you."

Silently she followed him down the passageway and into the other cabin.

The first thing Cimarron saw as he entered the room was the pile of money lying on the table between two wooden bowls. The second thing he saw was the log that had been removed from the flooring to reveal a hollowed-out portion of earth beneath where it had lain.

"Take a look at this," Tucson, who was seated beside Starr at the table, cried to Cimarron. He pointed to the paper money and the gold coins that Starr was counting.

Cimarron looked from the money toward Hall, who stood staring at Molly.

Hall slowly crossed the room and stood without speaking in front of his wife. He was about to embrace her, but when she cringed away from him, his hands dropped to his sides. Suddenly he spun on his heels and was about to lunge toward the table at which Starr and Tucson were seated.

Cimarron seized him and held him back. "We'll shoot

131

you, any one of us will, if you so much as breathe too loud," he said. "Now, I'm going to let you go, Hall. But you remember what I just said."

Tucson had slid his revolver from his holster and was almost idly aiming it at Hall. "Cimarron," he said, "you hungry? Molly there cooked us some food—stuff she called *sofka*—right after you left. What it is, it's hominy." He picked up a bowl from the table and offered it to Cimarron, who waved it away.

"Him and his goddamned money!"

Hall's sudden outburst took Cimarron by surprise. He turned to find the man gazing down at his dead father.

Through clenched teeth, Hall muttered, "He would never spend a cent he didn't absolutely have to spend. Not a single cent! He scrimped. He saved. For the future, he always said. Now look at him. He's dead." Hall suddenly lurched forward. His foot came up. He kicked at his father's corpse, which was lying on the floor at his feet. It rolled over and came to rest against the wall. Hall kicked at it again.

Starr didn't look up or stop counting the money piled on the table in front of him.

Tucson giggled.

Molly stood motionless at the entrance to the passageway, seemingly unaware of what was happening around her.

Cimarron went over to Hall and put a hand on the man's shoulder. "Take it easy."

As if Hall hadn't heard the words, he said, "All the years of hoarding his money like a squirrel scared stiff of the winter it knew was coming. All the days in all those goddamned years! And now this. He's gone. And soon his money will also be gone."

Hall turned slowly around and his eyes came to rest on his wife. "Molly—didn't you try to fight him off?"

"She fought Sam when he came after her," Tucson volunteered. "But by the time it was my turn, the fight was all gone out of her."

Hall began to sob, his eyes still fixed on Molly.

Her expression didn't change. It remained blank. There was a grim lifelessness in her black eyes.

"More than twenty thousand damned dollars," Starr

suddenly shouted gleefully. "Would you have guessed the old man had so much?" he asked no one in particular. "Belle will do a Copenhagen jig when she sees all this!" He waved his hand to encompass the money spread out on the table.

Cimarron glanced at Molly and then at Hall. Both of them need comforting, he thought. But neither was able to comfort the other. Not now, they weren't. Would they be able to do so in the days that lay ahead? he wondered. He hoped so.

"Let's go," he said sharply.

Starr's merriment instantly evaporated. "*I* give the orders, Cimarron. We'll go when I say we go."

"Have it your way, Starr."

"Let's go," Starr said, his voice still sharp. Then he smiled broadly at Cimarron.

Tucson took a cloth sack down from a shelf and began to stuff money into it. When he had filled a second sack, he handed one to Starr and, carrying the other, started for the door.

Starr, swinging the sack Tucson had handed him, followed Tucson out of the cabin.

Cimarron headed for the door. He wanted to look back. He didn't.

As they boarded their horses after Starr and Tucson had deposited the sacks containing the money in their saddlebags, Cimarron heard a sound from the cabin. He turned to look back at it and then yelled, *"Look out!"*

Hall stood in the cabin doorway. In his hand was the rifle that Cimarron had seen hanging on the wall of the cabin. Hall fired it.

But Starr fired at the same instant.

Hall's shot missed.

Starr's didn't.

Hall slumped across the threshold.

The last thing Cimarron saw before turning his horse was Molly, who had appeared in the doorway, her empty eyes staring down at the dead body of her husband.

He cursed as he rode through the night after Starr and Tucson. He had warned Hall not to try anything. Just give up the money, he had told the Creek. Don't do anything foolish. Well, Hall had done something foolish. He had gone for his rifle.

But was what Hall had done really so foolish, Cimarron asked himself, holding an arm up to keep low-hanging branches away from his face as he rode through a heavily wooded area. Was a man foolish to seek vengeance against the men who had murdered his father and raped his wife?

No answer came to him on the wings of the wind that was blowing noisily through the dark night.

He made a deliberate effort to try to forget what lay behind him and brace himself for what he knew lay waiting for him not far ahead in the deceptively calm night.

The plan he had conceived and explained to Hall at the busk would not now be able to help Hall, but it still might help Molly and Beatrice.

If it worked.

Starr rode through the trees to the left several minutes later as the flames of the busk's bonfire made the moon blush.

Cimarron turned his horse to the left and began to follow Starr.

Suddenly the night erupted in a cacophony of sound.

Shrill shouts in the Creek language tore through the air.

A Creek dropped from a tree branch and took Tucson out of his saddle. As the two men hit the ground, Starr managed to draw his revolver, but before he could fire it at any of the shadowy figures leaping from the trees where they had hidden themselves because of Cimarron's earlier instructions, a Creek who was perched on a low branch swung the hickory stick he had been using in the ball game and Starr's gun was clubbed from his hand.

Almost at the same moment, another hickory stick was swung by an invisible attacker. It struck the neck of the horse Starr was riding and the animal screamed and threw Starr to the ground.

As a Creek dropped from a tree onto the rump of Cimarron's dun, he saw Tucson scramble to his feet and fire.

A Creek spun around, his hickory stick falling from his

134

hand. He stumbled a few steps and then fell heavily to the ground.

Cimarron tried to elbow the Creek behind him off the dun's rump. He was rewarded for his efforts by a sharp blow from the man's hickory stick; it caught him on the side of the head and sent sheets of flickering white light burning through his brain. He lost his grip on the reins, and bathed in the sparkling white light that seemed to surround and swallow him, he felt himself sliding out of the saddle.

He hit the ground hard, rolled over, and reached for his Colt.

Two Creeks sprang toward him. One raised his hickory stick.

Cimarron rolled to one side, got his knees under him, and leaped to his feet. He reached out swiftly, seized the descending hickory stick, and wrenched it from the Creek's hands.

He swung it in a wide arc and heard it hit flesh and then shatter bone. One of the two Creeks went down, crying out his agony to add to the shouts and screams that were flooding the suddenly frantic night.

As the other Creek lunged toward him, Cimarron again swung the stick in his hands, but the Creek came in under it and butted Cimarron hard with his lowered head. The blow tore the breath from Cimarron's lungs. Before he could recover from the attack, the Creek ripped the hickory stick from his hands and raised it.

In a guttural whisper, the man said, "Show your shoulders."

Cimarron knew what the Creek intended to do. He turned slightly and tensed.

The hickory stick crashed down upon his shoulders and he went sprawling, his arms and legs flung out, on the ground that was wet with dew. He didn't move.

As the Creek raced away from him, Cimarron turned his head slightly.

Tucson, he saw, was battling hand to hand with a Creek. Starr was being held at bay by another Creek who had Starr's revolver in his hand.

Several Creeks were busy unstrapping the saddlebags from the three horses.

Tucson downed his attacker with a vicious right upper-cut and then he jumped the Creek who was holding the gun on Starr. But the Creek, eluding Tucson, turned and fired at him.

Tucson went down, a portion of his skull blown away.

Starr moved in on the Creek, but when the man turned swiftly toward him, he backed off, his hands rising until they were above his head.

Sudden silence filled the woods.

And then one of the Creeks shouted something Cimarron didn't understand because the Indian had spoken in his own language.

An argument broke out among the attackers.

Cimarron used the diversion to slither stealthily along the ground, making as little noise as possible, toward a spot he had picked out earlier as he lay on the ground pretending to be unconscious. The trees growing in the spot he had selected were thick, a tangled mix of oaks and poplars.

When he had reached the trees and gotten to his feet, he flattened himself against the largest oak and drew his Colt.

A moment later, the argument among the Creeks ended and silence returned to the woods.

The man holding Starr's gun cocked it.

"Don't!" Starr yelled. "Take the money, but don't—"

Cimarron fired at the Creek who was about to kill Starr and his shot knocked Starr's gun out of the Creek's hand.

"Run, Starr!" he yelled, and fired two more shots, which were deliberately aimed above the heads of the men clustered near Starr.

The shots scattered the gunless Creeks.

Starr raced toward his horse.

One of the Creeks raced after him.

Cimarron put a bullet into the ground just ahead of the pursuing Creek, who dived for cover in the underbrush.

Cimarron ran to his dun and leaped into the saddle. Gathering up the reins, he rode straight toward the few Creeks who had not taken cover, scattering them and yelling for Starr to follow him. He turned in the saddle as he rode and fired again, although no one was pursuing him.

Starr was just behind him, but a moment later he was galloping ahead of him as fast as his horse would travel.

Cimarron slapped his dun's flanks and the animal shot forward, its mane flying, its ears erect.

Ten minutes later, both men slowed their horses.

Cimarron studied his backtrail. He saw no one behind him, and had expected to see no one. Pursuit by the Creeks had not been part of his plan. But then, neither had murder been a part of the plan, but one Creek had tried to kill Starr. And Tucson had been killed.

"They got it all," Starr exclaimed, his voice heavy with disappointment. "They took my saddlebags and Tucson's."

"Mine too," Cimarron said, "though they got no money from mine. You want to ride back and see if we can take that money away from those Creeks?"

"Hell, no! There must have been at least twenty of them against only the three of us. Did you see what happened to Tucson?"

"I did."

"That Creek blew his brains out!" Starr swore.

So did Cimarron—but silently. Tucson's death had definitely not been a part of the plan.

When he had gone over it with the ball players before leaving the busk with Hall, he had ordered them not to kill either Starr or Tucson. But Tucson was dead.

Cimarron became aware of the pain in his shoulders where the Creek had clubbed him, as planned, with the hickory stick. He wished the man had not played his part in the affair quite so well. His right shoulder felt as if it had been dislocated.

But all in all, he thought, things had gone fairly well. The Creeks had retrieved the money stolen from the Halls, which was exactly what Cimarron had wanted to accomplish. And he had wanted it to happen without himself being suspected of having had a part in organizing the attack.

"What I want to know," Starr said suddenly, "is why those Indians bushwacked us. They must've known we were carrying Hall's money. They went for the saddlebags like they knew the money would be in them."

Cimarron said nothing.

Starr glanced at him. "Hall must have alerted them at the busk. You think he did?"

"Don't see how he could have," Cimarron said, thinking fast. "I didn't let him out of my sight for a minute. There was no way he could have— Wait a minute! He could have alerted them! Just before we rode out for the cabin, he said he wanted to say good-bye to his wife. He talked to her in Creek. That must have been how those young bucks knew what we were planning to do. Hall told Beatrice and she, after we'd gone, told them."

Starr's eyes narrowed. "You mean to say you went and told Hall what we were planning to do?"

"Sure I did. I had to. How else was I going to get him to come back to the cabin with me?"

"You mean you told him I killed his daddy?"

"No, I didn't tell him that," Cimarron lied. "But I showed him the piece of Molly's dress that Tucson gave me before I left. Up till then, Hall didn't believe what I told him about us intending to steal the money. When he saw that calico, well, then he believed me."

"You should have gotten him away from there without telling him a damned thing. You should have cut him out of that herd at the busk and then used your gun to force him to go with you."

"Maybe I should have."

"*Maybe I should have,*" Starr said shrilly, mocking Cimarron. "Just you wait till Belle hears how you messed us up. You'll be lucky if all she does is hand me a bull and order me to whip that white ass of yours to shreds!"

10

"You mean to tell me that you two came back here empty-handed?"

Belle had shouted her question at Cimarron and Starr as they stood before her in her hotel room in Tulsey Town. She placed her hands on her hips and looked disbelievingly from Cimarron to Starr.

"Why?" she shouted, her irritation blossoming into rage. "Tell me why!"

"Belle, calm down," Starr said. "What happened—well, it was like this."

As he began to explain what had happened after he and the others had stolen the money from the Halls, Belle's expression grew darker. She began to shake her head as Starr droned on, his eyes on the floor.

When he had finished his account of the events that had befallen him and the others, Belle barked, "You two are as empty-headed as you are empty-handed!"

"Now, Belle—"

"Shut up, Sam! It's the truth. You had over twenty thousand dollars in your saddlebags and you let a few savages take it away from you."

"I told you before, Belle," Sam said, scowling. "Don't call us Indians savages. We're not. At least, those of us from here in the Nations aren't."

"You Cherokees," Belle countered angrily, "could take a few lessons from the Comanches. No Comanche would have let himself be bushwhacked by a bunch of boys. A bunch of *ball players!*" She threw back her head and roared with bitter laughter.

When her mirthless laughter died, she turned to confront Cimarron. "You never should have told Hall what had gone on at his cabin. Sam was right before when he said you should have gotten him away before he had a chance to set up his little game. You're a fool, Cimarron!"

"Reckon I am, Belle," Cimarron said. "But not so much of a fool that I'll make the same mistake a second time."

"Can you give me a guarantee of that?" she shot at him.

He shook his head. "But I can guarantee you I'll be twice—*thrice* as careful the next time out."

"Is there any way we can get that money back from those bushwhackers?" Belle asked.

"If you've got enough men," Cimarron said, "maybe we could get it back from them. But I doubt it. The big problem, as I see it, would be finding the Creeks and the money. Not an easy job, no matter how many of us went looking."

"I think I know what they planned to do with the money," Starr said, excitement in his voice. "If I'm right, we've got no problem—none at all."

Both Cimarron and Belle stared at him.

"If Cimarron had the deal figured right," Starr continued thoughtfully, "if Artus Hall did tell his wife that Cimarron had told him about what was going on back at the cabin, and if Hall's wife then went and told the young bucks so they could set up an ambush——"

Belle interrupted him. "Sam, I think you've hit on it. That's what happened, that much seems clear. And I think I know what you were going to say next. You think the Creeks jumped the three of you to get the money back so they could return it to the Halls."

"That's what I was getting at," Starr confirmed. "But that might not be the way it worked out in the end."

"What do you mean?" Belle asked.

"Maybe those bushwhackers decided to keep the money for themselves," Starr said.

"I'll bet they did," Cimarron said quickly, disliking the way things were going and fearing where they might be leading. "The Halls would never know the difference if the bucks kept the money for themselves. They'd think we still had it. The Creeks could claim they weren't able to get it away from us."

Belle folded one arm across her waist, propped her other elbow against it, and slowly stroked her chin. "I think Hall had his wife set it up with his friends to jump you and get his money back. I also think they turned the money over to Hall's wives."

"If they didn't," Cimarron said, "we'll never run them all to ground, no matter how many of us go out after them."

"One thing is certain," Belle said with determination. "It's well worth a try to see whether or not the Hall women got the money back."

Cimarron suppressed a groan, waiting for what he knew was coming next, an image of the blank-eyed Molly darting through his troubled mind.

"Sam," Belle said, "you and Cimarron will go back to Hall's cabin. You shouldn't have any trouble with Hall's wives. Take Devlin and Pierce with you just in case you do run into any more trouble. We've got to act fast."

"How fast?" Starr inquired.

"You'll ride out tonight."

"Our horses are tired," Cimarron protested, trying to think of a way to change Belle's plan, trying to find a way to convince her that the Creeks had stolen the money for themselves and not, as she correctly believed, to return it to the Hall women.

But before he could come up with anything, Belle said, "There's another good reason why we've got to move fast on this matter."

"What's the other reason?" Starr asked.

"There's a deputy marshal in town from Fort Smith by the name of Renquist," Belle replied. "The boys spotted him and told me he was here. In fact, he's staying right here in the hotel.

"Sam, I'm leaving town and going to your ranch until things quiet down and that marshal moves on. After you and the boys have gotten the money, ride to the ranch. We'll rendezvous there instead of here."

Renquist, Cimarron thought, hope stirring within him. If he could get to Renquist before heading for the Hall cabin . . .

"I've got to see to my horse," he told Belle. "He needs feed and he ought to be rubbed down if he's to be in shape for our ride tonight."

"Meet Sam and the other boys at the saloon at seven o'clock tonight," Belle ordered him. "And . . . Cimarron . . ."

He was already halfway to the door, but when she spoke his name, he turned to face her.

"Don't fail me this time, Cimarron."

"I won't," he assured her, experiencing a sinking feeling in the pit of his stomach as he thought about Molly and Beatrice Hall and what lay ahead for them during the coming night because his plan to ensure the return of the stolen money to them had suddenly gone sour.

But as he left the room and made his way down the steps to the lobby, the hope he had felt earlier upon learning that Marshal Cass Renquist was in town grew within him and he began to believe that he still had a chance to get the drop on the Reed gang.

He went directly to the desk in the lobby and asked the clerk for the number of Renquist's room.

When the clerk gave him the number, he recrossed the lobby and climbed the steps, hoping he would not run into Belle or Starr. He could think of no way to explain to them if he did meet them what he was doing in the hotel. He certainly didn't want them to find out that he was on his way to talk to a lawman.

Renquist's room, he discovered, was only two doors away from the one Belle occupied. As Cimarron reached it and knocked on the door, he kept his eyes on Belle's door, ready to move away fast if it opened.

It didn't, but the door to Renquist's room did.

Cimarron pushed past Renquist and into the room, slamming the door behind him.

"What the hell—" Renquist blustered.

"Keep your voice down," Cimarron ordered him.

"Cimarron it's you," Renquist exclaimed as Cimarron turned to face him. "What are you doing here? Are you still trailing that witness Fagan sent you out after?"

"That man's dead."

"Then what are you doing here in Tulsey Town?"

142

"Sit down, Renquist, and listen to me. I haven't got a whole lot of time to tell you what I want you to know."

"Tell me."

Cimarron told Renquist as briefly as possible about all that had happened, concluding with the simple statement, "I need your help."

"Glad to give it, Cimarron. How many men will be riding with you tonight?"

"Starr and two others named Devlin and Pierce."

Renquist's right hand rose and began to finger the badge he wore on his vest.

He's nervous, Cimarron thought as Renquist idly fidgeted with his badge.

"Two against three," Renquist mused. He smiled. "Not such bad odds, I'd say." He paused a moment and then added, "I'm out here after a bootlegger. But that can wait. What you've got to wrap up is far more important than any bootlegger. I can go after him once we've caught Belle's boys. By the way, is there any chance of catching Belle herself?"

"Not likely. She's getting out of town. She's heading for Starr's ranch till things cool down. After we leave the Hall cabin, we're supposed to meet her there. I gather she doesn't go out on jobs like this herself. She's the brains behind the outfit. She plans things and then sends her boys to carry out her orders."

"That ambush was a pretty smart idea of yours," Renquist commented. "I'm not sure I'd have been able to come up with anything half as slick as that."

"It wasn't all that slick. And anyway, Belle's been smart enough to trip me up. But with your help, Renquist, we still might be able to pull the fat out of this particular fire."

"How do you want to go about it?"

"First of all, you've got to keep out of sight. But you've got to make sure to spot us when we ride out tonight for Hall's cabin so you can keep on our backtrail. Not too close, but close enough so you can catch my signal. When I give it, you ride in and the two of us'll get the drop on the others before any one of them can make a move or any harm can come to the Hall women."

"What kind of signal are you planning to give me?"

143

"I'll take off my hat and scratch my head. Do you think you can spot me in the dark?"

"The moon's nearly full. Sure, I can."

"You're a pretty good tracker, are you?"

"I'm not a modest man so I'll tell you that I could track a coon tiptoeing through a canebrake."

"Well, all I can say is that I sure am glad you turned up here when you did. I might have been able to manage things by myself, but at the moment I haven't got any notion as to how I might have done it. Renquist, I couldn't be gladder to see you than if this was Christmas Eve and you were Santa Claus."

"What happened to your witness?" Renquist asked.

Cimarron had almost forgotten about Archie Kane. Remembering the man now, he also remembered Lila and found himself wishing he were back at her cabin instead of where he was.

"Didn't you hear me, Cimarron?"

"Yeah, I heard you. I was just thinking. Kane was bushwhacked by somebody."

"You don't know who killed him?"

"Nope. And I don't know who it was who bushwhacked me neither."

"*You* were bushwhacked?"

"Not long after you brought me the message that Fagan wanted to see me—to send me out after Kane, as it turned out. I went to see Fagan when I left you and then I rode out. I'd gotten only as far as the foothills of the Boston Mountains when somebody with a rifle took a shot at me. To this day, I can't figure out why."

"Pete Smithers."

At first, Cimarron didn't recognize the name. But then he remembered Smithers. "You think because I had that fight with him back on the Arkansas that he turned around and tried to kill me?"

"Well, I saw the shape he was in when you got through whipping him. Mind you, now, I'm not accusing Deputy Smithers of anything. But I'm also not accusing him of harboring any special goodwill toward you. Not after the harm you did to him."

"He wanted a fight. I gave him one."

"I know. But you strike me, Cimarron, as a man who might have made a few enemies in your time."

"A few, I reckon."

"Well, you'd better watch your step. Whoever shot at you might still be out after you."

"I'd best be getting out of here now. Take a peek out in the hall. It wouldn't do for me to run into Belle or her man, Sam Starr. Not coming out of this room, it wouldn't."

Renquist went to the door and opened it a crack. He quickly closed it again. Turning to Cimarron, he said, "Belle's out there in the hall talking to someone. You'll have to wait till they go."

Cimarron went to the window, looked out, and then pulled aside the curtain covering it.

"What are you doing?"

Instead of replying, Cimarron climbed through the window and stepped out onto the hotel's overhang. He walked to one end of it, crouched, and jumped down to the street. As his boots hit the ground, his knees bent and he almost lost his balance. But he didn't. Straightening, he casually strolled into the hotel, intending to down a good hot meal in the dining room. He didn't know, he thought ruefully, when he'd get his next one—hot or cold. It was going to be a long ride across mostly unsettled land from the Hall cabin to Fort Smith with the three prisoners he and Renquist would find themselves shepherding before the night was over.

As dusk descended on Tulsey Town, Cimarron tethered his horse in front of the dry-goods store and then went around to the saloon where Belle had told him to meet Starr.

As he entered the raucous room that was filled with men drinking and playing cards, he immediately spotted Starr seated at a table near the bar.

The two men with Starr looked to Cimarron like hard cases. Both were bearded. Both were wirily built. Both had eyes—one set blue, the other brown—that were as cold as a copperhead's.

Starr raised a hand in greeting and Cimarron crossed the room and said, "I'm ready to go if you are."

"You've got time for a drink if you want one," Starr

told him. Without waiting for a response from Cimarron, he picked up the bottle that sat on the table and filled his empty glass.

Cimarron watched him down the whiskey and immediately refill his glass.

Starr offered him the bottle.

"No, thanks." Cimarron sat down in an empty chair.

"You're the fellow calls himself Cimarron?" asked the blue-eyed man in a flat voice.

"That's me."

"So this is Belle's brand-new gun," the brown-eyed man remarked in a voice that whiskey had coarsened.

Starr pointed to the blue-eyed man. "Devlin." Then to the brown-eyed man. "Pierce."

"Glad to know you," Cimarron said, thrusting out his right hand.

Neither Devlin nor Pierce made any move to shake it, so Cimarron withdrew it. "Friendly fellows," he commented to Starr. "They make a man feel real welcome."

Devlin and Pierce merely stared unblinkingly at Cimarron.

After Starr had once again emptied his glass, he rose. "Let's go. We've got a ways to ride."

He paid the bartender and then the four men made their way out of the saloon and around to the false-fronted dry-goods store, where their horses waited for them.

They boarded their mounts and rode out of town in a silence that remained unbroken for several miles before Devlin commented, "Nice night for a robbery."

"Any night is," Pierce amended.

Cimarron shifted in his saddle and looked back over his shoulder.

"You afraid somebody's backtrailing us?" Starr asked him.

"Nope. But I like to keep my eyes open and seeing in all directions. Gives me a sense of security to know what's going on all around me."

"Suspicious fellow, ain't he?" Devlin asked, and Pierce answered, "What makes him so fidgety, do you suppose?"

Starr laughed lightly.

Cimarron began to feel uneasy. Not only because he

146

had not caught sight of Renquist as he rode out of town, but also because he had a feeling that his companions were taunting him. Not that he minded. He'd taken his share of taunting along the trails he had ridden. But this was, in some strange way, different. The three men he was riding with seemed to find him—he searched for the right word and found it—amusing.

He forced himself to put his disconcerting thoughts out of his mind. He was probably a little bit spooked, he decided, because of what would soon be happening. That had to be it.

But his uneasiness grew as they rode on and Devlin began to talk about the time he had spent in a Texas jail after having been arrested by the Rangers for his free and easy use of a running iron to blot brands.

And as Pierce began to reminisce about how many men he had gunned down in his career as a hired gun.

"How about you, Cimarron?" Starr asked. "Tucson told us you rode with a gang down in Texas. Want to tell us about that?"

"Nope."

"Ever have any trouble with the law?" Starr persisted. Cimarron didn't answer the question.

"And he went and called us unfriendly fellows before," Devlin remarked, shaking his head in chagrin.

"The pot's got no right calling the kettle black," Pierce grunted.

They covered several more miles in silence.

Cimarron wanted to look behind him for some sign of Renquist, but he didn't.

They were moving through sparsely wooded country that was fairly level, although occasionally the land rose slightly and then dipped down again. Stars packed the sky. The three-quarter moon rode herd among them.

"Not much farther," Starr said some time later.

Only a few minutes after he had made his remark, Cimarron saw the light in the Hall cabin window, a small spark glowing in the moonlit night that was filled with stark and silent shadows.

Starr held up a hand and they halted. "Devlin," he said, "you go around to the left. Pierce, you circle to the

147

right. Cimarron and me'll wait here till you both get back."

As Devlin and Pierce rode away, Cimarron sat his saddle, his hands clasped around his saddle horn. Beside him, Starr stared at the quiet cabin.

"You think the money's really in there?" he asked Cimarron.

"Hard to say. It might be and then again it—" He didn't get to complete what he had been about to say because a rifle shot rang out.

He had seen no flash of fire. But he did see Pierce come riding hard around the left side of the cabin and, a moment later, Devlin came into sight on the right.

Another shot sounded.

Cimarron turned his horse and made for the shelter of the nearest trees. He could hear Starr's horse coming up fast behind him. Once in among the trees, he dismounted and pulled his Winchester free of the boot.

Starr dropped down from his horse and took up a position near Cimarron. "Who the hell's shooting?" he muttered.

Cimarron didn't know and didn't bother to say so. It seemed unnecessary.

The light in the cabin went out.

"Where's Pierce and Devlin?" Starr asked. "I don't see either one of them nor their horses either."

Neither did Cimarron. He supposed they had taken cover when the shooting started. He surveyed the terrain around the cabin, his rifle raised and ready. It was mostly flat. Here and there a poorly defined ridge rose halfheartedly. Trees were scattered about, the moonlight drowning in their branches.

He stiffened as he saw a figure dart out of the darkness and head toward him. He raised his rifle and sighted along its barrel.

It was Pierce.

"Creeks!" Pierce shouted as he bounded in among the trees. "At least one of them, maybe more. I saw one. What happened to Devlin?"

Before Cimarron or Starr could answer him, another rifle shot shattered the silence.

Another figure materialized in the night, rising up from

148

the ground and running fast toward the spot where Cimarron and the others had taken refuge.

"Don't shoot!" Starr snapped, knocking the barrel of Pierce's six-gun down. "It's Devlin!"

Devlin didn't make it to the trees.

Cimarron saw a spurt of flame on the far side of the cabin.

Devlin staggered and then fell as he was hit in the leg. "Cover me!" he screeched, and began to drag himself along the ground toward the trees.

Cimarron, although he had no specific target in his sights, fired at the spot where he had seen the flash of flame.

At the same instant, someone else fired.

A strangled cry tore through the night.

"I can't see to shoot," Pierce cried, but he nevertheless fired over the head of Devlin, who was still crawling slowly toward the trees.

Cimarron reached down and dragged Devlin out of the open. He helped him sit up against a tree and then he squinted across the moonlight-strewn ground in front of the cabin.

"That scream came from over there," he said, pointing to the left side of the cabin. "I figure there's two gunmen out there. We must've got one of them. Pierce, where'd you see the Creek?"

"I saw one who shot at me as I rode around the cabin. I saw him almost as plain as day."

Devlin said, "There was at least one more off to the other side. He got off a shot at me."

"That one's down, like as not," Cimarron said. "But maybe not dead. I'll circle around and come in from the other side. Somebody ought to do the same for the Creek on this side of the cabin."

"I'll do it," Starr volunteered, and moved out.

So did Cimarron.

He followed his backtrail for long minutes and then began to move at right angles to it, circling, listening carefully for any sound that was being made by something other than creatures native to the night.

He heard none as he began to circle back again.

Minutes later, he found the Creek. The man was on the

149

ground, a bullet wound in the back of his head. There was little left of his face where the bullet had exited.

Shot from behind, Cimarron thought. But this Creek had been facing us. Renquist, he thought hopefully.

"Cimarron!"

Cimarron spun around, rifle up, finger on its trigger.

"It's me. Don't shoot!"

Cimarron recognized Renquist's voice. "I can't see you."

Renquist rose from behind some undergrowth. "You okay?"

"I am. Did you kill this Creek?"

"Came up behind him. But there's at least one other one out there somewhere—back in the direction you were firing from."

"Starr's tracking him."

As a rifle barked twice in the silence, Cimarron added, "Maybe he's got him."

"Or maybe the Creek got Starr."

Someone shouted in the distance. Cimarron recognized Starr's voice.

"I got the bastard! I killed him! Cimarron!"

"Better answer him fast," Renquist advised.

"This one's dead too!" Cimarron yelled back, and heard Starr whoop with joy.

"Whenever you're ready, Cimarron," Renquist said.

"We'll move in on the cabin now. I'll drop back a bit. You come in behind us. Just before we get to the cabin door, you step out and join me so we'll have the drop on them."

"I'm ready."

"Forgot something," Cimarron said. "Devlin. He won't be able to walk. He's shot in the leg. You'd best position yourself so you can keep him in your sights too."

"How'll it be if I come in from behind Devlin's position?"

"Good idea."

"Cimarron," Starr shouted, "come on, dammit!"

Cimarron left Renquist and began to sprint toward the cabin.

Starr was waiting for him out in the open. Pierce stood beside him.

"Let's go," Starr said. "We got two women to visit inside that cabin."

"And a whole lot of money to visit too, I hope," Pierce said, grinning.

As they walked toward the cabin, Cimarron slowed his pace until he was several steps behind them. He carried his rifle at hip level, its barrel aimed at Starr and Pierce, who were talking softly to each other.

Just before they reached the cabin door, around which thick shadows crouched, Cimarron said, "Hold it, Starr! You too, Pierce!"

Both men abruptly halted.

Starr started to turn toward Cimarron.

"Face the door," Cimarron commanded. "Drop your guns and raise your hands."

Both men silently obeyed the commands.

"Renquist!" Cimarron shouted.

"Yo!"

Cimarron stepped backward and glanced to the right.

Renquist was riding a big black slowly toward him. In front of him, Devlin crawled along the ground, favoring his wounded leg.

Cimarron waited as the minutes passed and then Devlin was sitting on the ground in front of him as Renquist, smiling broadly, got out of the saddle.

"It worked," Cimarron said to him matter-of-factly.

"It did," Renquist agreed. "But not quite the way you figured it would."

Cimarron stared at him in disbelief as Renquist swung his rifle around and aimed it straight at him.

Starr and Pierce dropped their hands and picked up their guns.

Devlin looked up from the ground at Cimarron and began to laugh.

11

Devlin's laughter ended abruptly as he bellowed, "We got the drop on you, lawman!"

Cimarron's eyes darted from Devlin to Renquist, who was grinning and nodding his head.

"What the hell do you think you're doing, Renquist?" he asked, his voice loud in the otherwise quiet night.

"What's it look like I'm doing?"

"You're throwing in with these bandits?"

"No."

"Then what the *hell*—"

"I threw in with Belle and her boys a long time ago," Renquist explained. "Long before I first laid eyes on you back on the bank of the Arkansas. Get his guns, Pierce."

Cimarron's mind whirled as Pierce stepped forward and took his rifle away from him and slid his Colt from its holster.

He stared at Renquist, remembering the day the man had come to him in the deputies' camp and told him that Marshal Fagan wanted to send him out on a case. What was it that Renquist had said that day? Something about Fagan wanting him to bring in a witness to testify at a trial. Renquist had professed not to know any of the details of the case.

"Renquist," Cimarron said coldly, "you knew who Fagan was sending me out after, didn't you?"

"I knew, all right. He told me he was sending you out after Archie Kane so that Kane could testify against Dade Munrow."

"You and Fagan were the only ones who knew what my assignment was," Cimarron said. "And it wasn't

Fagan who had a reason to bushwhack me. It was you who fired at me from the Boston Mountains."

"Sure, it was."

"You wanted to kill me to keep me from finding Kane so the Munrow case would fall to pieces."

"It was Belle's idea," Renquist said. "She had me get myself a deputy marshal's job a year ago so I could keep tabs on what was going on in Judge Parker's court. From time to time, one of her boys gets himself arrested by a brave lawman like you. Belle's good at getting her boys out—one way or another. Either through hiring the best lawyer she can find to defend them or by getting one of her friends back in Washington to intercede with Parker. Or, as in the case of Munrow, by killing the only witness against him."

Cimarron said, "She told me she'd sent a man named Cory out after Kane. She said Cory hadn't come back."

"Oh, Cory came back, all right," Devlin said, and erupted again in laughter.

"And when he did, the jig was up for you, Cimarron," Pierce added.

Cimarron found that the conversation was making no sense to him, none at all. What did the man named Cory have to do with him? What had Pierce meant by saying the jig was up because of Cory? He didn't know the man. Did the man know him?

"Before Kane died," he said slowly, addressing Renquist, "he tried to tell me who killed him. It was night and the moon and stars were in the sky. Kane pointed at the sky. I didn't know what he was trying to tell me until I heard about Sam Starr. Then I thought maybe Kane was pointing at the stars to say that it was Starr who had shot him. But I knew that couldn't be the case when Belle told me she'd sent somebody named Cory out to kill Kane." Cimarron was about to go on, to continue trying to work things out in his mind, when he noticed Renquist idly fingering the badge that was pinned to his vest.

Suddenly it all became clear to him. "Kane *did* point to the stars!" he said. "I know now what he was trying to tell me. He was trying to tell me that a lawman had killed him. A man wearing a tin badge in the shape of a star!"

Renquist grinned.

"*You're* Cory!" Cimarron declared.

"That happens to be one of the names I go by," Renquist admitted cheerfully.

"When you didn't manage to kill me to keep me from bringing Kane in," Cimarron went on, "you went after Kane and killed him to keep him from testifying against Munrow."

"Too bad you didn't figure that out sooner," Renquist said. "If you had, you wouldn't be in the spot you're in right now."

Cimarron silently cursed himself for not having been able to decipher the dying Kane's cryptic message earlier.

"Belle was on to you," Renquist told him.

"We all were," Pierce declared. "Once Renquist here came back to report to Belle that he'd done for Kane and she mentioned you, he told her you were a lawman."

"I don't get it," Cimarron said truthfully. "If Belle knew I was a lawman, why didn't she have one of you kill me the way Renquist killed Kane?"

"Oh, Belle has a sense of humor," Renquist answered. "When I told her you came to me and wanted me to help you round up some of her boys, she decided to play along with your scheme, knowing it wouldn't work once the chips were down like they were a little while ago."

"Kill him!" Devlin snarled.

"I'm fixing to do that very thing," Renquist responded, raising his rifle.

"Hold it," Pierce said. "Wait'll we get ourselves out of the way, in case you miss. Come on, Starr! Let's go get our hands on that money that's been on my mind so long."

As Starr moved toward Pierce, Pierce reached out and pulled open the unlocked cabin door. He stepped over the threshold, Starr on his left.

In the darkness inside the cabin, fire flashed from the muzzle of an unseen gun.

Pierce spun around, his arms flailing the air. He staggered back toward the threshold, stumbled over it, and fell to the ground, his fingers clawing dirt, a faint moan issuing from between his lips.

Renquist fired.

But not at Cimarron. He fired into the black interior of the cabin.

A second shot came from within the cabin.

Starr ran.

Cimarron dropped to the ground and rolled. He struck Renquist's lower legs and Renquist fell over him, dropping his rifle as he went down.

Cimarron shoved him out of the way and seized the rifle he had dropped before Renquist could recover himself and retrieve it. He was up and running in an instant. As he flattened his back against the cabin wall, he saw Devlin dragging himself away from the cabin door.

As Devlin's hand closed around Cimarron's Colt, which Pierce had dropped along with Cimarron's rifle when he had been shot, and Devlin raised the six-gun, leveling it at Cimarron, Cimarron fired Renquist's rifle.

Devlin's body leaped and then slumped down upon the ground, Cimarron's Colt still in his hand, his body unwinding until he lay flat on his back, blood flowing from the small hole in the center of his chest.

Renquist was getting to his feet.

"Over there," Cimarron said to him, and pointed with the rifle.

As Renquist ran to the spot a few feet in front of Cimarron and out of the line of fire of whoever was in the cabin, Cimarron said, "Stand real still or I'll fix you so's you won't ever move again."

Renquist remained rigid.

Cimarron looked down at Pierce. It was obvious that Pierce was as dead as Devlin now was.

"You!" Cimarron shouted. "Inside the cabin. Don't shoot!" He identified himself and then reminded whoever it was inside the cabin about the ambush he had arranged with the Creeks at the busk. "I'm on your side," he shouted. "I'm a deputy marshal."

No sound came from inside the cabin.

"Molly!" Cimarron shouted. "You in there? Beatrice Hall? Somebody answer me!"

Light suddenly spilled from inside the cabin. It was followed by the sound of a man's voice. "If you are who you claim to be, show yourself."

Cimarron hesitated, his eyes on Renquist. He glanced

around him. Something was wrong. What? Starr! He realized that the man was missing. An instant later, he heard the sound of a horse galloping away into the night.

"I've got a prisoner out here," he yelled to the man inside the cabin. "I'll walk him in first. Don't shoot him. I'm taking him back to Fort Smith to stand trial for murder. Once we're inside, you can get a good look at me. You agreeable?"

"Come in slow."

"You heard the man, Renquist. Step out and on into the cabin."

Renquist, his eyes wide with fright, shook his head. "No," he murmured. "You saw what happened to Pierce. If I so much as show a toe in that doorway, it'll be blown off."

Cimarron's finger squeezed the trigger of the rifle he was holding and a bullet bit into the dirt in front of Renquist's boots. "If you don't do like I said, I'll blow *all* your toes off—every last one of them!"

The sweat on Renquist's face gleamed in the silvery moonlight as he moved slowly to the left; then, taking a deep breath, his hands held high above his head, he moved into the light pouring across the cabin's threshold. He stepped into the cabin and halted just inside the door.

But he moved on when Cimarron's rifle barrel jabbed him in the small of his back.

Cimarron entered the cabin behind him to find a lamp burning on the table—and the room empty.

He heard the soft whisper of sound as Renquist exhaled with relief.

"What the hell?" he muttered to himself, looking around. He glanced to his right. The passageway that led to the adjoining cabin was empty. His body suddenly stiffened as he felt the muzzle of a gun rammed into his back. He remained silent, standing rigid, as the gun was removed from his hand by whoever was standing behind him. Starr, he thought. He's got me dead to rights.

"Move over there to the far side of the room."

It wasn't Starr who had spoken. Cimarron recognized the voice of the man who had been in the cabin earlier.

Renquist moved first and Cimarron followed him across the room.

"Both of you—turn around slow. Keep your hands high."

Renquist turned around. So did Cimarron.

He recognized one of the Creeks who had been involved in the ball game at the busk, and almost sighed with relief. The man was one of those who had ambushed him and the others as they rode away from the Hall cabin after the robbery.

"Glad to see you again," he said to the man whose name he didn't know. "You sure do have a mistrusting nature."

"I went out the window behind you," the Creek said solemnly. "I thought it wise to play it safe."

"You believe me now?" Cimarron asked him.

"Can you prove you're a lawman?" the Creek inquired bluntly.

"If you'll let me, I'll drag my badge from my pocket and show it to you." When the Creek nodded, Cimarron did.

"That doesn't prove you're a lawman. There are all kinds of ways you could have gotten your hands on that badge."

"True enough. But do you think I arranged to have you men jump us last time we were here just for the fun of it? Do you think I was holding a gun on this man for the fun of it?"

"I guess you're telling the truth." The Creek lowered his revolver but he didn't return it to the holster that was hanging against his hip.

"Where's the money?" Cimarron asked him, lowering his arms.

The Creek's Colt came up fast.

Cimarron's arms reached for the sky even faster. "I was just curious, is all."

"Gone."

"Molly and Beatrice Hall?"

"Gone too."

"If I ask where, will you blow me to kingdom come?"

"They and their money are safe at a neighbor's house not more than a mile from here. We figured somebody just might come back and try a second time to steal the

157

money—and use the women the way they used Molly before."

"So you all set up a welcoming party?"

The Creek smiled.

"You know my name. You mind telling me yours?"

"Robert Harjo."

"You wouldn't happen to be kin to Echo Harjo, the Creek chief, would you?"

"He was my grandfather. You knew him?"

"Nope. But I heard about him and how he helped settle the differences between the Caddo and Wichitaw some years back by calling Colonel Upshaw on the carpet over the way he was dealing with the Caddo."

"That, Grandfather used to say, was a bad time."

"A bloody one too, I heard tell. The Caddo damn near wiped out the Wichitaw, and probably would have, were it not for men like your granddaddy. Now, I like talking over old times, but I figure maybe I better get busy taking my prisoner here back to Fort Smith."

"Go ahead."

"I'd be obliged if you'd ride along with us. I know the court would welcome your testimony about what happened here tonight as well as what happened the last time me and some others visited this cabin. As a matter of plain fact, it would be helpful if Artus Hale's wives were to come along with us too. I'd like it fine for the court to be able to listen to them tell what went on. One man got away tonight—Sam Starr. The United States marshal in Fort Smith will send somebody out to catch him, and the testimony of the Hall women will help convict him of rape and robbery."

"I'll have to go and get my horse. I walked here along with the other two men who met you outside. They're dead?"

"Starr killed one of them. He killed the other—shot him in the back." Cimarron nodded in Renquist's direction.

Harjo's eyes darkened. "They were good friends of mine. I'll be happy to ride to Fort Smith with you and talk to the court about him."

"We don't need to go to your place for your horse. There's two riderless mounts out there somewheres. You can ride one and lead the other. Now I think it's high time we got out of here and went to talk to the Hall women to see if we can get them to come with us."

Cimarron marched Renquist outside, and when Harjo came out of the cabin, he handed Renquist's rifle to the Creek. "Hold this on him."

Cimarron bent down and retrieved his rifle and Colt. After leathering the six-gun, he said, "I'll go hunt up those horses and be right back."

Cimarron was back in a few minutes, riding his dun and leading the horses that had belonged to Devlin and Pierce. "Renquist, get aboard your black. Harjo, you take one of these mounts and see to it that the other one tags along with us. Which way do we head?"

Harjo answered, "East."

They rode out a moment later, Renquist in front with Cimarron right behind him, rifle in hand, and Harjo bringing up the rear and leading the riderless mount.

No one looked back at the bodies of Devlin and Pierce lying in front of the cabin, two thick shadows among so many others that were equally lifeless.

When they reached the small house that had been their destination, Cimarron started to get out of the saddle, but Harjo gestured and he remained where he was as the Creek said, "It would be better, I think, if I speak to them."

He went to the door and rapped on it, calling out something in the Creek language. He waited a moment, rapped again, and called out in Creek again.

A lighted lamp appeared in one of the windows. A curtain was drawn aside and a man peered through the window. The curtain fell back. A moment later, the door opened.

Cimarron heard a whispered conversation in Creek, which he didn't understand, and then the door closed again.

"What's the matter, Harjo?"

"Nothing. We will wait."

They did.

Nearly an hour later, the door opened again and this time Molly and Beatrice stepped out into the night.

Cimarron's eyes were on Molly. Her face was paled by

the moonlight falling upon it, but her expression seemed alert. The blank-eyed look was gone. She nodded when she recognized Cimarron.

He touched the brim of his hat to her as a wagon clattered around the side of the house and stopped. The man who had been driving it got down and then helped the two women to climb aboard it.

Beatrice took the team's reins and, without a moment's hesitation, slapped them against the rumps of the horses.

The wagon moved out.

"This way!" Cimarron said, and pointed southeast.

Beatrice turned the team and followed him and Renquist. Again, Harjo brought up the rear, Renquist's rifle laid across his saddle, as the five people moved toward the horizon, above which the sky was gray with the dull light that preceded the dawn.

The sun was almost down when Cimarron finally called a halt.

"What are we stopping for?" Harjo asked him.

"You see that little cabin and shed off there near the horizon?"

"I see it."

"We'll stop there for a spell. Give the horses a rest. Let them graze."

"You're sure of a welcome, I take it?"

"I happen to know the lady who lives there," Cimarron answered. "Her name's Lila Kane."

Renquist twisted in his saddle and looked back at Cimarron.

"Renquist," Cimarron said, "I thought you might like to tell Lila what you did to her brother."

"I'm not going anywhere near her," Renquist snarled.

"Oh, yes, you are," Cimarron said quietly. "Move out, Renquist."

Renquist hesitated briefly and then reluctantly obeyed Cimarron's order.

When they were still almost a hundred yards from the cabin, Cimarron yelled to Renquist. "That's far enough!"

Lila, her Sharps in her hands, had appeared in the cabin doorway.

"Harjo!" When the Creek rode up, Cimarron said, "You

watch Renquist while I ride down there." He pointed to the cabin.

As Harjo dropped the reins of the horse he had been leading and trained his rifle on Renquist, Cimarron trotted toward Lila.

When she recognized him, she leaned her Sharps against the wall of the cabin and ran to meet him.

"Well, will you look what the cat dragged in!" she exclaimed as she reached his side. "You don't look any the worse for wear since I saw you last!"

"Hello, Lila. It's real good to see you again. How's your gunshot wound?"

"All healed. Who's that bunch out there?"

"A Creek by the name of Robert Harjo. The two women are also Creeks. The other man's name is Renquist. Part of the time. He's been known to call himself Cory too."

"Harjo's holding a gun on him. Why?"

"Because he tried to kill me." Cimarron paused briefly before adding, "He's the one who killed Archie."

Lila raised a hand to shield her eyes as she stared in silence at Renquist, who was looking away from her.

"Let's go on to the cabin." Cimarron walked the dun toward it, and a moment later Lila began to follow him on foot.

He turned in his saddle and waved the others on. At the cabin, he dismounted and said, "You been missing me, Lila?"

When she didn't answer him, he turned around and saw her running, Sharps in hand, toward the approaching party, which was being led by Renquist.

Cimarron immediately sprinted after her.

Up ahead of him, Lila dropped to one knee and raised her rifle.

Cimarron threw himself upon her, knocking the Sharps from her hands and flattening her against the ground.

"Let me up!" she screamed. "I'm going to kill that bastard as sure as the sun sets in the west!"

Cimarron straddled her and held her tightly by the wrists as she struggled against him. He told her to calm down, to take it easy. Several times.

When she finally stopped struggling, he released her and stood up.

"It's all right," he called to Harjo and the women.

But it wasn't.

Lila was up off the ground and running.

Before Cimarron could reach her, she had seized Renquist and pulled him out of the saddle. The two of them were rolling over and over on the ground when Cimarron reached them. He made a grab for them, but they rolled away from him.

"Dammit, Lila, stop fussing!" he shouted at her.

She sprang to her feet, pulling Renquist up with her. Holding him by his shirt, which she clutched with her left hand, she drew back her right fist and let it fly. It landed squarely on Renquist's jaw, knocking him backward.

He fell.

Lila leaped on top of him.

Renquist tried to fight her off, but his efforts were ineffectual; she pummeled him with both fists and then began slamming them hard against both sides of his head as she held his squirming body tightly between her knees.

Cimarron reached out and grabbed her shoulders. He pulled her up and away from Renquist, and as he did so, she turned swiftly and brought up her right knee, which struck him in the groin.

He let out a howl of pain and doubled over, clutching his genitals. Then he hobbled as fast as he could after Lila, who was running back toward the spot where her Sharps lay in the grass.

She reached the rifle before Cimarron could reach her, and as she swung the barrel up, aiming at Renquist, who was struggling to his feet, Cimarron raised his arms to block her shot.

"Damn you, Cimarron!" she screamed at him.

He hobbled toward her, seized the barrel of the rifle, and wrested it from her. "Now you cut this out, woman, or I'll—I'll—"

"You'll what?" she shot at him angrily, her eyes afire as she stood with her hands planted firmly on her hips.

The sight of her furious face and belligerent stance was suddenly too much for Cimarron. He doubled over again. This time in laughter. And then, straightening, his free left hand buried between his legs, he said, "Honey, you damn near went and gelded me back there with that nasty knee of yours."

"You should have minded your own damn business!"

"Lila, honey, Renquist is my business. Now, you know that. I'm taking him back to Fort Smith to stand trial for killing Archie, among other things."

"I'm going with you."

"You're not. Renquist's life wouldn't be worth a bent penny with you along."

"I'll behave."

Cimarron shook his head. "I'd as soon believe the promise of a painter not to kill the heifer he's caught in his claws."

"Give me my gun."

"No." Cimarron turned and watched the others ride warily in. When they reached him, he said, "We'll let the horses graze. Lila, get them some water. Harjo, you guard Renquist. Would you ladies like to step down and stretch your legs?"

"I'll find something for us to eat," Lila said, and headed for the cabin.

Cimarron, remembering the meal she had cooked for him during his previous visit, decided he wasn't hungry.

As he leaned Lila's rifle against the cabin wall and started toward his horse, Molly came up to him and said, "I want to thank you for helping us the night—" She dropped her eyes.

"I was glad to do what I could. I just wish it could have been more and better."

"Come along, Molly," Beatrice said, taking her by the arm.

Cimarron watched the two women enter the cabin and then he went to his dun and loosened its cinch strap. He raised his saddle slightly and adjusted his saddle blanket to air the animal's back.

After tightening the cinch, he went to where Harjo stood with his rifle trained on Renquist. "Go get yourself something to eat. After you've eaten, bring a plate out here to him."

Renquist said, "I wouldn't eat any grub that woman cooked for me. She's liable to put poison in it."

"Get off your horse," Cimarron ordered Renquist as Harjo went toward the cabin. "You can sit down in the shade of his shadow if you've a mind to."

"Now that's real thoughtful of you, Deputy," Renquist said as he got out of his saddle and sat down on the ground beside his horse.

"Not thoughtful at all. Just plain practical. I want you to stay in good shape till we get to Fort Smith."

"Well, if that's what you want, you'd better keep that Kane hellcat far away from me."

Cimarron began to feel a growing sense of impatience as time passed slowly and the sun set. He wanted to be on his way, but the more he thought about the journey that lay ahead, the more he realized he would probably be better off making camp here at Lila's cabin for the night. The Hall women would be more comfortable under a roof, he reasoned. But he also knew that they would all be spending at least one night in the open before they reached Fort Smith. Well, that couldn't be helped. They would all set out before first light in the morning, he decided.

When Harjo appeared with a plate of food for Renquist, Cimarron told him what he had decided and Harjo made no objection. Leaving Harjo to guard Renquist, he went to the cabin.

Lila persuaded him to eat, which he did—lightly because once again the sowbelly she had fried was nearly charred—and then the two of them left the cabin together.

As they stepped over the threshold, a rifle shot rang out and Cimarron saw the rifle fly from Harjo's hands. The shot, he believed, had come from behind the cabin.

"Get back!" he ordered Lila as he unholstered his Colt and began to move cautiously along the cabin's front wall.

Behind him, Lila let out a furious yell, grabbed her Sharps, and went running out into the open.

Cimarron silently damned her foolishness and then he saw why she was running.

Renquist was climbing back into the saddle of his black.

Another rifle shot sounded, and as Lila leaped aboard Cimarron's dun and went galloping after Renquist, Cimar-

164

ron rounded the corner of the cabin and found himself confronting a mounted Sam Starr.

Starr fired at him, but Cimarron dodged the shot. He brought up his Colt and fired. His bullet bit into Starr's arm. Starr wheeled his horse and galloped away. Cimarron fired at him again, but missed. He would have fired a third time, but he realized that Starr was well out of range.

He was about to run back to get his Winchester from the saddle boot when he remembered that Lila had taken his dun.

He spun around and saw her standing up in the stirrups of his saddle and swinging her Sharps by the barrel as she pursued the fleeing Renquist. He saw her overtake Renquist and he saw the stock of Lila's rifle strike Renquist on the shoulders and send him flying out of the saddle.

Molly and Beatrice suddenly appeared in the doorway of the cabin. One of the two women screamed. Cimarron didn't know if it had been Molly or Beatrice because his eyes were fastened on Lila, who had halted his dun and was aiming the Sharps at Renquist, who lay on the ground staring up at her.

Cimarron was about to shout to Lila, to order her not to shoot, when he saw her lips moving. He watched Renquist get up from the ground and gingerly climb back aboard his black.

Lila moved him out and followed him back to the cabin.

"Starr almost pulled it off," Cimarron said to Renquist when the man rode up to him. "He must've been trailing us."

"Did he shoot you?" Lila asked.

"Nope. I winged him, but he got away from me again. Looks like we're all going to have to keep a sharp eye out for him from now on."

"*I'm* going to keep a sharp eye out for *you*," Lila announced, her eyes on Cimarron. "You could have got yourself all shot to pieces just now. And lost your prisoner, into the bargain, if I hadn't of been around."

"I don't need any looking after," Cimarron said rather sharply because of his disappointment over Starr's escape.

Lila gave him a sly smile. "You don't? None at all? Of any kind?"

"Well, maybe a little of one kind or another now and then," he replied, matching her smile.

Starr did not put in another appearance during the remainder of the journey to Fort Smith.

When Cimarron and the others finally reached the town, they headed immediately for the stone-walled compound and the courthouse squatting inside the enclosure.

Once inside the compound, Cimarron dismounted and ordered Renquist out of the saddle.

"You know the way to the jail," he told his prisoner, and as Renquist headed for the door set in the side of the courthouse, Cimarron followed him, his rifle ready in case Renquist decided to make a break for it.

Faces in the windows of the basement jail watched the pair's progress. Cimarron tried to ignore them, remembering the time he himself had recently spent locked up in that filthy hellhole. But he found it hard to ignore the desperate faces of the imprisoned men as they continued to stare wordlessly at him, despair or defiance reflected in their eyes.

As they passed the gallows, Renquist glanced up at it.

"It's waiting for you," Cimarron told him.

He also gave the gallows a glance and recalled how close he himself had come to standing up there on that wooden platform beneath the sloping roof, one of George Maledon's oiled nooses around his neck, his hands bound behind him, and a black hood draped over his head while he waited for the trap to open beneath his boots so that he could fall and his neck be broken. . . .

He shuddered.

Renquist halted in front of a door. Behind it, Cimarron knew only too well, was the corridor that led to another door and the huge basement room in which prisoners awaiting trial—or execution—were housed.

"Knock," Cimarron ordered.

Renquist reluctantly did.

"Hello, Burns," Cimarron said to the man who unlocked and opened the door. "Brought you a prisoner."

"Where is he?"

"Why, Charlie, he's standing right in front of you."

"I don't see anybody but Deputy Renquist."

"He's the prisoner I'm talking about." Cimarron gave Renquist a shove.

As Renquist stumbled into the corridor, Burns gave Cimarron a puzzled look. "Marshal Fagan said he sent you out to bring in a witness and here you come with one of our own. What's going on, Cimarron?"

"The witness I was after is dead. Renquist killed him. Now you go and lock him up tight and I'll go and report to Marshal Fagan."

Burns closed the door and Cimarron made his way back to where the others were waiting for him. "Molly, you and Beatrice and Harjo come along with me. I want you to tell Marshal Fagan all that happened."

"What about me?" Lila asked. "Don't I get to describe what I saw happen?"

"Lila, you wait right here," Cimarron told her. "Hang on to my horse for me. I'll be back before you can start feeling lonesome."

He shepherded his three witnesses up the steps of the courthouse and into the building, where he led them to Marshal Fagan's office.

He knocked on the office door.

"Come in," Fagan roared from behind it, and as Cimarron and the others entered the office, he spluttered, "A man can't have a moment's peace in this place so he can get some work done. Now what— Oh, it's you, Cimarron. Who are these people?" He jabbed a finger in Harjo's direction. "That's not Archie Kane. Kane's not an Indian. What's going on here, Cimarron?"

"If you'll keep still for a bit, Marshal, I'll be glad to tell you."

"All right, all right! I'm listening!"

Cimarron described everything that had happened to him from the time Renquist had tried to bushwhack him until he had captured Renquist at the Hall cabin.

Then he asked the Hall women and Harjo to tell what they had experienced, and they did—Beatrice boldly, Molly reluctantly, and Harjo eagerly.

When they were finished, Fagan sighed and said, "I wish it weren't true. I trusted Renquist." He slammed a fist down on his desk. "What's the law coming to if you can't trust its minions?" he asked rhetorically, and then sighed again and added, "I'm glad I'm getting out of this business."

"Getting out?" Cimarron prompted, wondering what Fagan meant.

Fagan gave him a woebegone look. "I'm quitting. Two years in this job is enough for any man. At least, it is for *this* man."

"Who's taking over as marshal?" Cimarron inquired.

"D. P. Upham. Fine man. Judge Parker recommended him and President Grant appointed him. Well, I wish Upham luck and I'll see to it that he issues warrants for the arrest of Myra Belle Reed and Sam Starr. Would you like to be the one who goes out after them, Cimarron?"

"I would—only not right this minute, if that's all right with you, Marshal, on account of I've got somebody waiting on me outside."

Fagan's eyebrows arched. He got up from his desk, went to the window, and looked out. "I might have known it. Who is she?"

"Lila Kane."

"Archie Kane's wife?" Fagan turned around, disapproval etched on his face.

"Not his wife. His sister."

"Oh, I see. Well, that makes it—"

Cimarron didn't hear the rest of what Fagan had to say because he was already out of the office and, a moment later, out of the courthouse as well.

He went to where Lila stood waiting for him and took the reins of his horse from her hand. As she hooked her arm in his and they headed for the gate of the compound, Cimarron, leading his dun, asked, "You ready, honey?"

"For what?"

He told her, and she smiled and quickened her pace as they left the compound and headed for the Fort Smith Hotel.

SPECIAL PREVIEW

Here is the first chapter
from

CIMARRON
AND THE BORDER BANDITS

third in the new action-packed
CIMARRON series from Signet

1

The horse under Cimarron was tired but it plodded gamely on through the timbered countryside, the sunlight that filtered through the trees dappling the horse and rider.

"We've not got too much farther to go," he told the dun, and lightly patted its neck. "We'll reach the Texas Road we're fixing to travel down almost as fast as old Judge Parker back in Fort Smith can condemn a vinegaroon to death by hanging."

Cimarron was riding west and the surface of the Arkansas River on his right glistened in the sunlight. He abruptly turned his horse and headed it in a southwesterly direction, and as he did so, the trees—mostly blackjack and post oak—began to thin out and finally give way to open land that stretched out for some distance ahead of him.

As he rode across the savanna, the long grass growing

on it brushed some of the dust from his battered black boots, into which his worn jeans were tucked.

The sun that burned in the blue caldron of the sky, undaunted now by any trees, streamed down and both Cimarron and his dun were soon sweating. He found himself missing the coolness of the timberland he had left, and he suspected that his horse did too.

When he reached the Texas Road, he turned the dun to the left and rode south along it, the reins held loosely in his hand as he let the dun choose its path and pace as he walked it down the heavily rutted road.

His original destination had been North Fork Town, but he had changed his mind while riding through the timberland and had decided to head instead for McAlester in Choctaw Nation so that he wouldn't have to ford the north fork of the Canadian River.

Carefully folded and tucked into the pocket of his blue flannel shirt was the warrant Marshal D. P. Upham had given him the day before. He was to serve it on a Chickasaw named Tillman Spinks—if that turned out to be possible. It might not be possible, he knew. Spinks might remain out of the reach of the federal court in Fort Smith because Spinks might find himself sentenced to hang by the Chickasaw court in which he was to be tried for having shot and killed another Chickasaw.

Marshal Upham had warned Cimarron not to serve the summons on Spinks if the man was convicted by the Chickasaw court. The warning had been unnecessary, but Cimarron hadn't bothered to tell Upham that. He knew that the greater crime of murder took precedence over the crime listed in the warrant in his pocket, which accused Spinks of having shot at—and missed—a white man. The murder, because it involved two Indians, was out of the United States court's jurisdiction. But the crime of shooting at a white man of which Spinks was accused was a matter for Judge Isaac Parker's court. It would, however, become a moot issue if Spinks was found guilty of murder by the court in Colbert in Chickasaw Nation, the court that was Cimarron's ultimate destination.

When McAlester came into view a little more than an hour later, Cimarron rode directly to the train depot, where he asked the stationmaster when the next south-bound train was due.

"It's due," the man replied, taking a watch from his pocket, opening it, and squinting through his spectacles at it, "in exactly forty-eight minutes. When it gets here—well, that's another matter entirely."

"Can you point me the way to a livery stable?" Cimarron asked, and when he had the directions, he thanked the stationmaster and turned the dun toward the town.

At the livery, he dismounted and led the dun into the stable, becoming aware as he did so of the strong smell of fresh manure, old leather, and damp straw. The smells, he thought, of civilization. Out in the open, the wind whips them away before most people can even notice them. But in here, he thought, they're prisoners and there's not much chance of them escaping.

"Help you?"

Cimarron nodded to the stableman who had approached him. "I'd be obliged if you'd let me feed my horse while I look him over."

"Help yourself. The grain's in sacks lined up against the wall back there."

When Cimarron had stalled his horse, he filled the feed trough with oats and then proceeded to strip his gear from the animal.

As the dun ate, he shook out his saddle blanket and draped it over one of the stall's walls to air. He got a clean cloth from the stableman and gently wiped the sweating animal down. He ran his fingers through the horse's mane and found it clean, but he discovered and removed several cockleburs from the animal's tail.

Talking softly to the dun, he lifted each of its feet in turn to examine its shoes. He found a nail wound in the left rear foot.

He left the stall and went to the stableman, who was lounging in the stable's sunny doorway. "You happen to have a thin piece of metal of some kind that I could use to dig a nail out of my horse's foot? Some pine tar, maybe, that I could use to treat a wound in his foot?"

Without a word, the stableman left the doorway and rummaged through his storage box. "This ought to do you," he said, holding up a small piece of tin. "And there's pine tar in this here crock."

"Much obliged." Cimarron carried the crock and piece of tin back to his horse and lifted the injured foot, which he placed between his knees. He slid the tin between foot and shoe and managed to work the nail loose. He used an index finger to daub pine tar on the puncture wound before placing the dun's foot back on the ground.

He found a pail, filled it from a water barrel, and then sat down outside the stall, his back braced against its wall, his forearms resting on his upright knees.

When his horse had finished eating, he got up and watered it and then returned to the stableman, who was still sunning himself in the open doorway.

"I could use a hammer and a nail."

When he had obtained both from the stableman, he proceeded to replace the nail he had removed from the dun's foot.

As he prepared to leave the stable, the stableman appeared and quoted a price. Cimarron paid it and swung into the saddle. He headed back to the depot and the small restaurant he had noticed that occupied one side of it.

After tying his horse to the hitch rail in front of the depot, he entered the restaurant and ordered coffee and stew.

The coffee was black and strong. The stew was watery and weak.

After finishing his meal, he paid the man sitting on a high stool near the door and went outside, where he found the stationmaster piling luggage on the platform from whom he bought a ticket. Several white men, all of them well-dressed, and two Indian women were waiting for the southbound train.

One of the dandies checked his watch. "Late again." He muttered an oath and the two women moved farther along the platform in an effort to avoid him.

The Missouri, Kansas, and Texas train, when it finally pulled into the depot, was almost twenty minutes late.

It consisted of two passenger coaches, two empty stockcars, a caboose, and a tender behind the locomotive which stood spouting smoke as two brakemen, one on each side, moved alongside the train inspecting its wheels.

Cimarron took off his black slouch hat and waved away the cinders that were falling through the air from the train's smokestack.

As the conductor stepped down onto the platform, Cimarron went up to him and said, "I'd like to load my horse in one of those empty stockcars."

"It'll cost you extra, you know."

"I know." Cimarron got his horse and led it over to the stockcar that was directly behind the second coach. After removing a book from his saddlebag, he unlatched and then slid back the slatted side of the car. He pulled the heavy wooden ramp from the car and braced it against the ground, positioning it at a slant, which allowed his dun to climb easily into the empty car.

He shoved the ramp back into the car, closed the door, reinserted the peg in the loop of the latch, and then, carrying his book, went to the nearest coach and climbed aboard.

He opened the vestibule door, which had a frosted-glass window, and stepped inside the coach, dropping down upon the red plush of the first empty seat he found. He leaned back, pushed his sweat-stained hat back from his forehead, and opened his book as the train rattled out of the station.

He was still reading when the train, whistling, pulled into the station at Atoka. He didn't look up from his book as the coach began to fill up with passengers.

But he did look up when the woman sat down next to him on the aisle side of his seat.

She was wearing a black grenadine dress with a taupe ruffle bordering its high neckline and the hem of its skirt. Over her dress, she wore a three-quarter-length fur cape. On her head was a sedate black bonnet. On her feet, she wore elastic-sided patent-leather shoes.

But it was not her clothes that interested Cimarron. What he found of interest was her striking young face, which he found almost beautiful, and her body, which he found decidedly voluptuous. As her right hip pressed lightly against his left one, he closed his book and set it aside.

Her face was calm, almost expressionless. No, he

thought, not calm—cold. On the haughty side, when you came right down to it. She struck him as aloofly aristocratic.

Above her broad forehead her hair—what he could see of it—was parted in the middle, and was as black as her bonnet. Her nose was aquiline and the full lips between it and her firm chin appeared to pout, which Cimarron found oddly provocative. Her smooth skin was tawny and he found himself reminded of the color of cougars. Her pronounced cheekbones looked to him to be as fragile as bone china and the rich color of her skin made her large eyes seem even blacker than they really were—two deep pools that stared straight ahead at nothing.

Chickasaw, probably, he speculated. Full-blood, he guessed, judging by the color of her skin and her eyes, which he wished would turn and look at him.

He looked down at her hands, which were holding her reticule, which rested in her lap. She was wearing black kid gloves, but he thought he could make out the impression of a wedding band beneath the leather covering her left hand.

"These seats are a bit snug," he commented as the whistle shrieked and the train rumbled out of the station and away from Atoka. "You got enough room?"

"I'm quite comfortable, thank you."

Her voice was as cool as her expression, and as controlled. She's not one to be easily rattled, Cimarron thought, though I wouldn't mind trying to rattle her some.

"That's good," he said. "You live in Atoka, do you?"

"No."

"You were visiting there, is that it?"

"No."

Cimarron decided to try a different approach, since she was obviously not interested in volunteering any information about herself. "Folks call me Cimarron," he told her, and then, when she continued to stare straight ahead, he said, "Since we're to share this seat for a spell, might I ask your name Miss—Mrs.—"

"Ada Barrett." She turned and looked directly at him. "*Mrs*. Ada Barrett."

Cimarron hadn't missed her emphasis on the word "Mrs." A warning? Maybe.

174

"I take it you're a widow?"

"I am, yes. These clothes I'm wearing—well, they do make my status rather obvious, I suppose."

"It's not just your clothes. I noticed that you didn't use your husband's given name when you told me your name. You said Mrs. *Ada* Barrett. Now, I figure a woman whose husband was alive probably would've used her husband's first name."

"You're a perceptive man, I see."

"I try to be. A perceptive man's likely to stay out of trouble, if you take my meaning." Cimarron gave her a grin.

"Yes, he is," she agreed solemnly, and looked away.

"Where're you headed, Mrs. Barrett?"

"Colbert."

"Well, now! So am I!"

Ada glanced at the book that Cimarron had stuffed between his right hip and the armrest panel. "I see you're a reader."

"I am when I can set aside some time for it." So she was interested in the fact that he read books? Well, it was as good an opening as any. He picked up the book. "This was written by a renegade named Thoreau back in the States. Its title is *Walden*."

"I've never had the opportunity to read *Walden*. Why did you call Mr. Thoreau a renegade?"

"Well, that's easy enough to answer. He doesn't think like most folks. Or act like them either. He goes his own way, and I have to admit I admire that."

She looked from the book to Cimarron's face. "You're also a renegade?"

"There've been some people I've met in my time who'd tell you I was."

"You haven't answered my question."

"Not real sure how to, Mrs. Barrett."

Instead of pursuing the matter, she asked, "What sort of books do you like to read?"

"No particular kind, I guess. I read just about everything I can lay my hands on, from Ned Buntline's dime novels and newspapers to what's printed on cans of tomatoes."

"You find pleasure in reading, I take it?"

Cimarron thought about her question for a moment and then leafed through his book. When he found the passage he had been searching for, he said, "Listen to this. It's from Thoreau's essay on reading. Maybe it'll answer your question for you." He quoted, " 'I aspire to be acquainted with wiser men than this our Concord soil has produced, whose names are hardly known here.' " He met her steady gaze. "That's what I aspire to, too. I'm always glad to get acquainted with people a whole lot smarter than I am. It's a good way to learn things you're not likely to learn any other way. Sure, you sometimes meet smart men on the trail or around a camp fire from time to time. But that's chancy. You're sure to meet them in books—just like Thoreau said. I like to learn from them—all kinds of things that set a man like me to thinking."

"I understand you perfectly and I should add that I share your thirst for knowledge."

"It's nice to have something in common with somebody like you," Cimarron commented, keenly aware of the heat of her thigh against his own.

"My people have always possessed a strong desire for learning—for education."

"Your people?"

"The Chickasaw. I know them well, of course, because I am one of them. But I am also aware of their strong desire to see their children educated from quite another point of view. A professional one, as it happens. I'm a teacher at Wapanucka Institute."

"That's a school west of Atoka, isn't it?"

"Yes, it is. We educate both girls and boys at the secondary level."

"What do you yourself teach them?"

"Greek and Latin."

"You know those languages?" Cimarron asked, awed.

"I can read and translate them, yes."

"Now, that is one fine accomplishment, that is. You know, I never had you pegged as a teacher, Mrs. Barrett."

Her lips parted slightly, but there was no warmth in her smile. "What did you have me pegged as?"

Cimarron, instead of answering her question, glanced, disconcerted, out the open window.

The train was entering a narrow cut that had been

176

gouged out of the heavily timbered hills that sloped steeply upward on both sides of the tracks.

Suddenly, the train slowed. Its wheel flanges shrieked as they ground against the rails.

As the train ground to an abrupt halt, Ada Barrett was thrown off balance. She fell heavily against Cimarron and he dropped his book.

"What's wrong?" she asked nervously. "Why have we stopped?"

Cimarron, his eyes on the two men loping out of the timber and running toward the train with guns drawn, leaped to his feet. "Excuse me, Mrs. Barrett."

"Where are you going? What's wrong?"

She received no answers to her questions because Cimarron had pushed past her and was running up the aisle toward the coach's vestibule.

Two men, he thought as he ran. There might be more.

He pulled open the vestibule door and then made a grab for the iron ladder that ran up the side of the coach. He quickly climbed it and, once up on top of the coach, scanned both sides of the tracks.

There was no one in sight.

No mail car, he thought. Which most likely meant that the train was carrying no money—other than what the passengers happened to have. So, he concluded, it's the passengers the jaspers plan to rob.

He began to run along the top of the coach, and when he reached the end of it, he leaped to the roof of the coach in front of it.

He slowed down as he neared the end of the coach and then dropped down and flattened himself on top of its roof. He eased his body forward, cautiously raised his head, and looked down on a scene in the cab of the locomotive, which did not surprise him because he had been expecting to confront it.

One gunman was holding the conductor, the engineer, two brakemen, and the fireman at bay, all of their faces, with the exception of the gunman's, which he couldn't see, lit by the flames from the open firebox.

"Drop it!" Cimarron shouted down to the gunman, his Colt .45 in his right hand.

The man whirled, his gun rising.

Cimarron fired.

The gunman went down, to writhe on the floor, his hands clutching his chest.

"Get his gun," Cimarron barked, and the conductor picked up the fallen gun and aimed it at the downed gunman.

Cimarron got up and climbed down the iron ladder. He damned the frosted glass in the vestibule door because it prevented him from seeing inside the coach. He reached out and whipped the door open.

One of the two gunmen in the car—the one at the far end of the coach—spotted him and yelled, "Look out, Ben!"

But Cimarron moved faster than Ben, and when he was directly behind him and his gun was pressing against Ben's back, he called to the bandit beyond him. "You shoot and Ben here's a dead man."

The other man hesitated, and Cimarron, using the barrel of his gun as a prod, moved Ben forward as frightened passengers cringed away from the pair. He wondered how many more bandits there were.

The coach was eerily silent, as if no one wanted to speak and possibly risk, by that act, the sound of lead burning its deadly way through the air.

Ben suddenly threw himself forward and hit the floor.

The other bandit fired at Cimarron, but Cimarron dived for cover into an empty seat. He heard the bullet bury itself in the wood of the coach's wall. At the same time, he fired and killed the man who had tried to kill him.

As Ben started to rise, Cimarron left the empty seat, put out a boot, and butted him with it. Ben fell forward. This time he lay facedown on the floor and he didn't move again.

"Any of you men got a gun?" Cimarron asked the passengers.

"I have," one of the men replied.

"Good. I'm a deputy marshal. See to it that this man doesn't get up off the floor till I get back."

He turned and raced back the way he had come. He went through the vestibule and leaped down to the ground. Bending low, he ran, his boots crunching on the gravel bed beneath him, along the side of the coach, keeping well below the level of the windows.

How many more men were there? He didn't know. But he did know that the sound of his shots would be likely to cause any others who might be in the second coach to investigate.

At the end of the first coach, he paused, and then, when he heard someone move from the second coach to the first, he vaulted up onto the small platform and quickly took in the situation. The door to the second coach was open. He saw no gunman inside that coach. But as he turned back toward the first coach, a shot sounded inside it and he saw the bandit who had just entered it crumple and hit the floor.

He nodded approvingly as he noted the thin curl of smoke rising from the barrel of the .45 in the hand of the passenger he had ordered to guard Ben.

"Don't you move, mister."

The voice, low and harsh, had come from behind Cimarron, and he obeyed the guttural order. He didn't move.

"Drop your gun," was the next command he received.

Reluctantly Cimarron let his Colt go and it fell to the floor.

The man behind him said, "Turn around."

Cimarron did, his arms rising.

"Now ease over to the left."

Cimarron hesitated. He knew what the gunman's order meant. He was about to be shot and the gunman didn't want to risk hitting Ben, who was inside the first coach, when he fired. But there was a chance, Cimarron thought. If he moved to the left—far enough and fast enough—his movement would open a line of fire for the passenger with the gun inside the first coach. That man, Cimarron hoped, might be able to bring down the gunman who was about to throw down on him.

He was about to make his move when he noticed a stealthy movement just behind the gunman. Someone was moving up on the gunman from inside the second car.

Stall, Cimarron told himself. "You don't have to kill me," he said to the bandit facing him. "You could let me go and get on with what you've been doing."

"Move, dammit, and move right now!" The gunman suddenly let out a yell as his hat flew off.

Cimarron reached out and wrestled the gun from the man's hand, turned quickly, and picked up his Colt.

As he straightened up, he saw her. "*You* slugged him?"

Ada Barrett smiled her mirthless smile and held up Cimarron's copy of *Walden*. "I did. With this."

As the gunman started to get groggily to his feet, he suddenly hurled himself against Cimarron.

But Cimarron was ready for him. He merely stepped backward, neutralizing the attack.

The gunman leaped from between the coaches and was off and running into the trees.

Cimarron got off a snapshot but missed his target.

The gunman disappeared in the timber.

A yell from behind him caused Cimarron to spin around.

The man named Ben had a grip on the wrist of the armed passenger and was battling the man for the gun he held.

It went off.

Startled, the passenger lost his grip on the .45 and Ben got it away from him.

"Get down!" Cimarron yelled to Ada Barrett, and then he fired.

Ben was knocked backward by the impact of the bullet. He tried to grab one of the seats, missed it, and crumpled to his knees as blood began to soak his gray shirt just above his waistband.

Cimarron waited, gun ready, eyes narrowed.

But Ben didn't fire again. He toppled to the floor.

Cimarron glanced out at the hill. No use going after the one who got away. The bandits had probably hidden their horses in among the trees. The man who had escaped was probably well away by now.

He turned around and saw Ada Barrett standing directly behind him. "I told you to get down."

"I did. But then I got back up again. Are there any more of them?"

"I don't think so. There were five of them. Three are dead in there." He pointed to the first coach. "One got away and one's wounded up in the cab. I've got to check on that one."

He entered the first coach and, edging around the three corpses that littered the aisle, moved on until he came to the cab.

"This man died," the conductor told him as he entered the cab. "May I ask who you are?"

"I'm a deputy marshal out of Fort Smith," Cimarron replied. He turned and retraced his steps.

With the help of several passengers, he removed the corpses from the coach and then ordered all the men out of the coaches and up to the front of the train to help clear away the pile of timber that had been laid across the tracks by the bandits to halt the train.

Once the track was clear and the train was again moving south, Cimarron made his way back to Ada Barrett.

He found her distributing the belongings that had been taken from the passengers during the attempted robbery. They were contained in a bandanna that had apparently belonged to one of the bandits.

Cimarron sat down in the seat he had left earlier, and when she resumed her seat beside him, he watched her slip the thick gold wedding band onto her finger, the ring that he guessed had been taken from her by one of the bandits.

"You took a chance doing what you did before," he told her.

"I didn't want to lose this." She held up her left hand and light glinted on the gold band on her finger.

"I thought you did it to help me out of a bad spot."

"I did it to help us all out."

"Well, you were a big help, that's for certain. I'd about come to the end of my rope when you slugged that jasper that was about to drill a hole or two in my hide."

"Frankly, I doubt that you'd reached the end of your rope. You behaved like an enterprising man who could have taken care of himself without any help from me."

"I thank you for the compliment."

"I didn't intend my statement to be a compliment. I was merely stating what I believe to be a fact." She opened Cimarron's copy of *Walden* and began to read.

Then, looking up at him, she said, "I am sorry. I seem to have appropriated your book."

As she offered to return it to him, Cimarron shook his head. "You go ahead and read it. Me, I'll try to get some sleep." Might as well, he thought, 'cause I can't seem to get past the barn door with this uppity widow woman.

He drew his hat down over his eyes, leaned back, folded his arms across his chest, and was soon asleep.

Ada Barrett woke him as the train pulled into Colbert depot.

She handed him his book and said, "I hated to wake you because you were sleeping so soundly. But I didn't want you to miss your stop."

"I thank you kindly, Mrs. Barrett."

"Good-bye." She hurried up the aisle and disappeared through the vestibule door.

Cimarron caught sight of her through one of the windows. She was climbing into a buckboard and he watched her take a seat beside a wizened old man, an Indian, who held the reins of the buckboard's horse in his gnarled hands.

As the old man clucked to the horse, it trotted briskly away from the depot. It rounded the corner of the depot and disappeared from sight.

Cimarron left the train. After getting his dun out of the stockcar, he asked a man lounging near the depot if he knew when Tillman Spinks was going to be tried.

"That trial's going on right now," the man informed him. "Has been for a day or two, if my memory serves me right."

"Where's the case being heard?"

"At the courthouse on the square in town. You'll find it easy. It's a one-story affair that somebody got the crazy notion to paint a robin's-egg blue. Don't ask me why."

"Much obliged." Cimarron stepped into the saddle and headed for Colbert's town square. When he reached it, he spotted the courthouse immediately. It was impossible to miss the pale-blue building sitting so sprightly among its drab neighbors.

After tethering his horse to one of the poles that supported its overhang, he went in and found himself in a large room that was filled with chairs for spectators, nearly all of them occupied. At a table set on a raised platform sat the judge. A man sat in a chair next to the judge's table. He was bathed in the light of the sun, which streamed through a window directly behind him.

Cimarron stood, arms folded, just inside the door, listening as the judge addressed the man standing in front of his table.

"Mr. Palmer, I'm sorry, but I cannot in good conscience grant you another delay. Defense counsel, as you have just heard, objects to such a motion, and he does so on what I consider to be sound grounds. You have already requested and obtained from this court two delays. But you have still failed to produce your witnesses against the defendant."

"Your Honor," began the harried-looking Indian who was obviously the counsel for the prosecution, "I am convinced that my witnesses have been intimidated during the past several days that this court has been sitting. Undoubtedly by cohorts associated with the defendant, Spinks."

Cimarron studied the man seated in the chair next to the judge's table. Spinks had a low forehead that was no more than a narrow band of dark flesh between his head of oily brown hair and his bushy eyebrows. He was unshaven and his nose seemed a misshapen lump in the center of his face. His brown eyes seemed dull, as if he were bored with the proceedings taking place around him. His lips were completely hidden by a drooping mustache. His skin was naturally dark but it had been made darker by the sun, which, with the help of the wind, had also seamed it.

The door beside Cimarron opened.

"Well, hello there," he declared as Ada Barrett hurried into the courtroom. "I thought you left town."

"I was leaving town when I learned that this trial was in progress, so I returned at once."

"No!" declared the judge loudly. "Counsel for the prosecution has been wasting the time of this court for the past several days as well as the money of our citizens, who pay to support it. The case of Chickasaw Nation against Tillman Spinks is hereby dismissed!"

Spinks, no longer bored or indolent, leaped from his

183

chair and shouted his delight at the dismissal of the case against him.

Cimarron thought he heard someone gasp. Had it been Ada Barrett? He turned his head and saw her swiftly draw a .32-caliber revolver from her reticule.

Before he could recover from his surprise, she fired.

Spinks' joyous whoops were replaced by a cry of pain as Ada Barrett's bullet tore into the flesh of his left shoulder.

About the Author

LEO P. KELLEY was born and raised in Pennsylvania's Wyoming Valley and spent a good part of his boyhood exploring the surrounding mountains, hunting and fishing. He served in the Army Security Agency as a cryptographer, and then went "on the road," working as dishwasher, laborer, etc. He later joined the Merchant Marine and sailed on tankers calling at Texas, South American, and Italian ports. In New York City he attended the New School for Social Research, receiving a BA in Literature. He worked in advertising, promotion, and marketing before leaving the business world to write full time.

Mr. Kelley has published a dozen novels and has several others now in the works. He has also published many short stories in leading magazines.

JOIN THE CIMARRON READER'S PANEL

If you're a reader of CIMARRON, New American Library wants to bring you more of the type of books you enjoy. For this reason we're asking you to join the CIMARRON Reader's Panel, so we can learn more about your reading tastes.

Please fill out and mail this questionnaire today. Your comments are appreciated.

1. The title of the last paperback book I bought was:
   TITLE:_____ PUBLISHER:_____

2. How many paperback books have you bought for yourself in the last six months?
   □ 1 to 3   □ 4 to 6   □ 7 to 9   □ 10 to 20   □ 21 or more

3. What other paperback fiction have you read in the past six months?
   Please list titles: _____
   _____
   _____
   _____

4. My favorite is (one of the above or other): _____

5. My favorite author is: _____

6. I watch television, on average (check one):
   □ Over 4 hours a day □ 2 to 4 hours a day
   □ 0 to 2 hours a day
   I usually watch television (check one or more):
   □ 8 a.m. to 5 p.m.   □ 5 p.m. to 11 p.m.   □ 11 p.m. to 2 a.m.

7. I read the following numbers of different magazines regularly (check one):
   □ More than 6   □ 3 to 6 magazines   □ 0 to 2 magazines
   My favorite magazines are: _____
   _____

For our records, we need this information from all our Reader's Panel Members.

NAME:_____

ADDRESS:_____

CITY:_____ STATE:_____ ZIP CODE:_____

8. (Check one) □ Male   □ Female

9. Age (Check one): □ 17 and under   □ 18 to 34   □ 35 to 49
   □ 50 to 64   □ 65 and over

10. Education (check one):
    □ Now in high school   □ Graduated high school
    □ Now in college   □ Completed some college
    □ Graduated college

11. What is your occupation? (check one):
    □ Employed full-time □ Employed part-time □ Not employed
    Give your full job title:_____

Thank you. Please mail this today to:
CIMARRON, New American Library
1633 Broadway, New York, New York 10019